FOREST OF THE SASQUATCH

4 REDEMPTION

LUKA T. JACOBS

Once a blade in another's fist,
now he learns the hand is his.

FROM THE AUTHOR

Well, here we are, fearless readers. The finale.

I never imagined *Forest of the Sasquatch* would grow into a full saga. What began as a single book quickly took on a life of its own, and I owe that entirely to you, the readers who connected with these stories.

This book tested me more than any other in the series. Telling so much of the story through Sasquatch eyes was both a challenge and a reward. Fiction lets me bend reality a little, but I still had to avoid slipping into easy human habits. I wanted their thoughts and speech to stay primal and raw. It stretched me as a writer in ways I didn't expect, but I guess we cannot truly grow without a challenge.

From Levi's desperate run for survival, to Rob's captivity and rescue, to Aluk's rise and fall, this series has explored it all. And now, it all leads here, to *Redemption*, the final chapter of the saga.

Thank you for walking this path with me.

Luka T. Jacobs

CONTENTS

PROLOGUE

Each footfall sank deep, pressing through the soft crust into the older, heavier layers below. The snow swallowed the shape of his steps, but the sound carried, a slow, grinding crunch that echoed through the trees like bones shifting beneath flesh. His wide feet flexed naturally over the uneven ground, the mid-tarsal break spreading with each stride, adapting to the slope and the weight of his movement.

Matto stepped through the treeline with slow movements. His chest rose and fell with exhaustion. His arms hung low, knuckles scarred and stained. One eye had swollen nearly shut. A deep gash ran down his thigh, stiff with blood and ice. Several bullet holes dotted his arms, the flesh torn and dark. In time, the metal would work through the skin and fall out, as it had before. Part of his left ear was missing, ripped away during the chaos. His body had held through the long return, but the fight had taken something harder to name.

A week earlier, Aluk had overpowered their elder and taken the clan. He gathered others from distant bloodlines and led a force east to strike the hairless ones in their great cluster of dwellings. Thirteen of their own did not return. Aluk did not return. Matto did not know how many from the other lines were lost.

He had grown beside Aluk since they were small. He had slept near him, learned his routes, matched his stride. When Aluk spoke, Matto listened. When Aluk moved, Matto followed. He had not always agreed with the way Aluk bent others to his will or turned fear into a tool, but the shape of that power lived in Matto's hands all the same. In the last rush against the hairless ones, Matto had watched Aluk die. He knew he had gone too far, yet he would miss him all the same.

As he stopped just outside the sanctuary's cave, he could hear the ones who had stayed. The wounded from a week before. The mothers with young. Six mothers remained, with their small ones, and three others, female and male, who had not been strong enough to follow Aluk east.

. He lowered into a crouch beside the mouth of the cave and sat. His arms draped loosely over his knees. His breath came slow and visible. He stared at the trees, unmoving.

From time to time, shuffling echoed faintly behind him. Those inside shifted, tended, watched. The wounded. The mothers. Their young. They had survived by staying behind.

Two mothers came to the mouth of the cave during the long stretch of morning. One held an infant on her hip. The other stepped out to scan the trees. She exchanged a short grunt with the first before returning inside.

Matto did not look at them. He did not acknowledge them.

He sat until the light shifted and the air grew colder again. His muscles relaxed, his gaze fixed on nothing.

High above, hidden in the trees that lined the cliff, Brak watched.

He left the sanctuary well after the clan and shadowed their trail through the snow. He helped stop one of them from hurting hairless ones, then returned ahead of Matto and stayed in the branches, silent. His auburn hair had collected snow across his shoulders. His breath showed in careful bursts. He studied Matto for a long while, his eyes following the way the older one held himself, tense, rigid, angry. Brak did not move. He did not approach.

His mother had remained inside the cave, tending to his

young sister, focused and quiet like the others.

Later that day, another figure returned.

Kara emerged from the east, her steps slow, her limbs weighed down by a tiredness deeper than skin. Scrapes marked her legs and arms, and a long scrape ran across her right arm where a bullet had grazed. Her hair was matted with snow, mud, and blood. She had not believed in Aluk's way; she had gone because there was no choice. Saying no meant being outcast.

She paused just beyond the clearing and sniffed the air. One of the mothers stepped out, exchanged a low grunt with her, then slipped back inside. Kara's eyes went to Matto. He did not move. She settled nearby and sat.

They didn't communicate.

That evening, while the forest stayed still, and the wind moved through the trees, Kara pressed snow-packed moss into the torn places along Matto's arms. Once the blood loosened, she wiped it away with her hand and chewed pine needles into a thick mash, packing the sharp-smelling pulp into the wounds. She tore bark from a fallen spruce and used the damp inner side to press it flat. He barely flinched. If he noticed at all, he gave no sign.

The sky dimmed. Night came with no change in position. Matto remained still. Kara stayed beside him. The wind brushed through the treetops, but the forest said nothing.

By the second day, it became clear no others would return. Matto had sensed it before then, but now it settled in his bones. Kara seemed to know it too. The mood across the sanctuary changed. Quieter. Slower. From the cave came only soft chattering and the low sounds of grieving, a hollow rhythm, the air gone thin.

The wounded inside stirred now and then, but not much. The mothers emerged only when needed. Matto did not move from his place before the cave mouth. Snow gathered on his shoulders and hair, crusted along his arms. Only the thin steam of his breath, lifting now and then, told Kara he lived. Without it, he was stone under snow. He didn't acknowledge the others. He did not eat. Kara gave him space.

Brak stayed out of sight, shifting from perch to perch. He waited.

On the third morning, hours before the light had started to rise, Matto stood. His grunt was harsh but low. Kara rose without hesitation and followed him into the trees.

They said nothing. They didn't look back.

Brak stepped out from the rocks not long after. He moved carefully, following their trail at a distance.

CHAPTER 1

Inside the cave, the air was thick with the stink of wounds and excrement. The wounded lay in clustered hollows near the back, their limbs sprawled over moss and stone, their bodies twitching or still. Some had begun to heal. Others had not.

Brak's mother, Runi, crouched near her daughter and touched the young one's cheek. She was three winters old, already strong in limb but tired now from hunger and stillness. Her skin was warm beneath Runi's hand. She stirred once, murmured softly, then curled tighter beneath her mother's arm.

Runi rose slowly and scanned the cave.

Six mothers moved among the injured, heads low, hands working without sound. They chewed bark and roots into soft paste, packed it into gashes that had refused to close. The wounds had come from the hairless ones' thundersticks or the blast of red breath that erupted from their strange metal tools. One male had a hole through his side. Another had a broken leg bent the wrong way and wrapped tight with wet hide and branch splints. A few responded to touch. One hadn't opened his eyes in days.

Runi moved toward one of the larger males, crouched low against the wall. His chest was broad, his face torn along the side, and blood had dried thick in the hair beneath his ribs. She reached for his side to replace the wrapping, but his arm shot up, sudden and forceful, and slapped her hand away.

She froze, eyes narrowing. He bared his teeth but did not speak.

Runi chattered back at him, low and rapid, her hands gesturing in short, angry movements. The other mothers turned to glance. She scolded him like a stubborn child, then pulled back and left him alone, chattering under her breath as she moved on to another.

No one made noise beyond what was needed. The wounded groaned without voices. The mothers didn't speak unless they had to. They cleaned and packed and moved on to the next.

One thing was clear; everyone was hungry.

The small ones clung to their mothers' sides or were buried beneath long arms, eyes half-shut, watching the dark with quiet unease.

Runi finished tightening a wrap around a swollen arm, then stood straight, stretching her back until her joints cracked. She looked towards the mouth of the cave and sniffed the air.

One slow inhale. Then another.

Behind her, two mothers glanced up. One gave a soft click, almost a whisper. The other stilled, ears turning toward the entrance.

Runi walked forward, eyes focussed and her steps silent. Her hand brushed the stone near the opening as she came to stand just before the entrance.

Moonlight filtered through the high branches and shimmered against the frozen trees. The glow sat faintly on the ground, soft and cold, touching the edge of the clearing with an uneasy stillness.

Beyond the clearing, between the trees, something watched.

Two eyes. Large. Set high. Fixed and amber-colored. Not reflection. Not light. They did not blink.

Runi's chest tightened.

She stared.

Her lips peeled back. Her throat rumbled.

The sound was low and heavy, a heated warning without hesitation.

Behind her, the mothers gathered their young.

More eyes joined it, pairs kindling between the trunks, high and still.

The eyes did not blink.

They only moved closer.

CHAPTER 2

As Matto led the way, he tasted the air, lifted his chin to the thin wind, and set his feet to the old line that ran from the sanctuary down into the river bottoms and cedar thickets where game held through winter.

He and Kara moved by habit. She would swing wide on the far side, reading wind and cover. He would take the near trail, cut sign, and push game back toward her. The moon was thin. Snow fell soft and steady.

Not long after leaving the sanctuary, he heard small feet behind him. He lifted his nose and sniffed the air. Young sweat. For something so small, he thought, he made a lot of noise. After a bend in the trail, he stopped. Brak, not looking up, walked straight into the back of him. It was like hitting stone, and Brak stumbled back.

Matto turned and showed his teeth. A low, rumbling sound came up from his chest.

He chattered sharply. *"You should not have come. Go back."*

He turned and went on as if the words were a rock set down. He did not look again.

Kara slipped in from a side path, set her hand on Brak's arm, and drew him a step off the trail.

She chattered, *"Listen. Learn. Stay low. Put your feet where the ground keeps its shape."*

Brak swallowed and nodded. He kept his voice soft.

He grunted, *"Yes."*

Kara pointed with two fingers to a snapped twig at knee height.

She chattered, *"This speaks when you should not speak. Do not break. Lift and pass."*

She set two fingers on his heel mark where it had pushed too deep.

She chattered, *"Do not move the earth. Touch and leave."*

They moved. Matto went ahead, a heavier shadow in deeper shade. Kara kept Brak a body's length behind her. When she stepped, he stepped. When she paused, he stopped and let his breath settle before it could find the cold and show itself.

They crossed a low dip where ice hid under new powder. The snow there creaked if a heel bit hard. Kara spread her fingers to warn him and stepped on the soft edge so the crust would not crack. She slid under drooped fir boughs and touched the tips so they would not shake loose snow onto his back. She knelt and showed him where a track had filled with powder until only a ghost of its shape remained, and how to see across it instead of down so the line through the trees would appear.

She chattered, *"Read edges. Read shade."*

The stink of deer came thin and true. Matto lifted his chin as Kara's hand tightened once on Brak's forearm.

She grunted, *"Stay. Watch."*

Matto slid ahead along the line, shoulders low, while Kara peeled off wide to take the wind right. Brak sank to a knee behind a fir trunk and held still. Through the branches he saw the deer ghost between trees, head high, ears cutting the air.

Matto edged left; Kara drifted right. They did not rush; they closed in by inches. The deer stepped faster, then broke into a run.

The forest closed ranks and then opened. Matto surged. Kara turned the animal with a low sound and a flash of arm. Snow flew from hooves. Matto took two heavy strides and struck, catching the hind leg with both hands and pulling the body sideways. The deer rolled once. Matto was on it with weight and will. He caught the head, one hand under the jaw and the other at the back of the skull, and wrenched. The neck broke with a dull crack. The legs kicked twice and went loose. He stayed one more breath, then another, until the body was still.

Brak did not move. He watched the way they had become a single shape around the kill, how each had known where the other would be without word. Matto rose. He set his palm to the still head. Kara touched the shoulder once and stepped back.

Matto lifted the deer and set it across his shoulders. He turned into the trees without looking at Brak. Kara came back to the fir and set her hand to Brak's. She squeezed once.

She chattered, *"See. Push. Turn. End quick."*

Brak acknowledged with a soft grunt.

They skirted a tangle of deadfall where new flakes whispered on bark. Kara tapped her ear and the air.

She led him back along their own soft marks, skirting where his heel had gone too deep before. Ahead, Matto's shape moved through fir shadow silently, the deer on his back, not looking back.

CHAPTER 3

They came back as the sun lifted a thin strip through the trees. As they neared the sanctuary Matto sensed something was wrong, not in trunks or snow, but in the air itself. Blood rode the scent. Death rode its shadow.

Matto slowed and raised his head, drawing the scent in deeply. Kara followed with Brak at her hip, her eyes gone hard. No birds called. The brush at the edge held still. No sounds came from the cave.

They crossed the last firs, and the clearing opened while feeling smaller than it should. The mouth of the cave stood black and still.

Matto dropped the deer, lifted his hand and grunted, *"Wait."*

Brak smelled the truth, his stomach falling as his feet carried him forward; he slid under Matto's arm while Kara reached, fingers grazing his forearm before he tore free.

She grunted, *"No."*

He did not stop. He slipped through the narrow mouth, the air inside carried a weight he had to push through. Blood and waste and hair, the sour reek of many bodies gone still. Splatter climbed the walls high and fell low; stone held a brown sheen where wet had dried. It was worse than the scent had said. Bodies lay everywhere, gathered in corners and strewn across open floor, limbs tangled on moss and rock. Necks bent wrong. Ribs folded where weight came down and kept coming. Faces swollen and slack. Throats crushed by hands. The floor told the rest: churned prints and heel gouges, knuckle blood smeared on stone, tooth marks in forearms, all of it saying they had fought until the body had nothing left and then more. It was all of them. The injured. The mothers. The young.

Brak went to the back where the roof dipped and the stone made a warm corner in the cold. Two bodies lay there. His mother held his sister even in death, her arms around the small ribs, her jaw set as if the hold might still protect her. Blood had matted their hair together. His mother's hands were bloody and cut, a clear sign she had fought to the end.

He knelt and set his cheek to his mother's ribs and waited for any lift. Nothing moved. The small chest did not rise, either. A sound rose in him, low at first and thin, then fuller, a ragged cry that shook his shoulders and wet his face. Whimpering, he lay down beside them, his arm over both, and did not move.

Kara stood just inside the mouth and took the carnage in until nothing new remained. She stepped back into the light. Matto came to the mouth, looked once, and went out with her. They sat at the cave mouth, shoulders to stone, saying nothing.

Inside, Brak cleared the small face of his sister with the back of his knuckles. He set his mother's and sister's hands together and pressed them flat so the stone would hold them both. He stayed with them.

Outside, the clearing kept its silence. Cold slid along the mouth and drew the cave's smell into the first light. Far off, a single coyote called once and went quiet. Within the cave held the weight of what had been done. It was total. It was ruin. It was the end of a home.

When the sun stood high, Matto broke the silence.

He chattered, *"They come again."*

Kara's eyes stayed on the trees.

She chattered, *"Why did Finland kin do this?"*

He replied *"Aluk took many of them. Their elder wants blood for blood. End all who live here."*

She chattered, *"Do we set them in the old way?"*

He replied, *"No time."*

He chattered, *"We put them in the hole where others went before. We leave before they return."*

They rose and went inside. Kara touched Brak's shoulder, gently.

She chattered, *"We must go."*

He did not answer.

Matto and Kara began to move the dead. One by one they lifted and carried, set each into the old deep hole at the back where they buried all of their kin. When it was time for Brak's mother and sister, he would not let go. Kara pulled him away, slow and firm. Matto lifted both together and lowered them into the hole, careful and steady.

At the cave mouth, Kara set both palms to stone and

bowed her head.

She chattered, *"Ancestors, take them. Old stone hold them. Old root keep. Old water carry their names."*

CHAPTER 4

Once it held a hundred heartbeats. Now it held the quiet of ruin.

As they left the sanctuary, the cold clung to them, turning their breaths into slow, faint clouds. Brak trailed behind at first, his steps dragging with the weight of his sorrow. Matto kept a steady pace, eyes always forward, never looking back. Kara moved lightly between them, her gaze shifting from trail to treeline as though expecting something to emerge at any moment.

Brak's mind wandered often in those first days. At night he would lie on his bedding and stare at the small breaks in the canopy, searching for the dim glow of stars. He thought of his mother and sister more in these moments than any other, remembering their scent and faces. Sometimes, as sleep pulled at him, he imagined the warm press of their shapes beside him, and for a moment the cold felt far away.

Matto noticed Brak drifting into their heat and let him stay. He had never kept a small one at his shoulder, had not asked for it, yet Brak stayed. If he was to walk with them, he would learn the quiet, keep clear of a hunter's path, and carry weight.

By mid-morning Matto slowed and then stopped so suddenly Brak almost walked into him again. The big one crouched and set his wide palm to the snow, and Brak leaned in where faint marks showed, small, delicate ovals running toward a tight knot of brush. Matto tilted his head, and a picture came into Brak's mind: *a hare flashing from cover, a Sasquatch still as stone, the coil before the jump. Wait.*

Kara slid away into the shadows, each step so clean the snow barely gave under her weight. She vanished into the thicket and came back with a limp hare hanging from her hand. No sound. No warning.

Matto shifted the other way and was gone a breath, then returned with a second hare, its neck slack in his grip. He sent another image across to Brak: *circle wide, keep wind right, break the run.* Kara slipped off once more and took a third with a quick grab in brush so tight it should have saved the small thing. It did not.

They set the three hares on the snow. Matto slid one toward Kara and pushed one toward Brak, keeping the last for himself. He tore his open and ate. Kara ate. Brak stared at his and did not touch it. His mouth went tight. He shook his head and grunted, *"No."*

Matto did not press and took the hare for himself.

By the next morning, the frozen ground beneath their feet sang with a low groan. Brak glanced down at the pale surface, as Matto crouched and studied the snow. Longer, narrower impressions marked the ground, with a faint drag line between each.

Kara chattered low, her tone edged with tension. *"Hairless ones. Two."*

The scent came to Brak then, sharp and bitter, like the tang left after stones struck too hard together. His brow furrowed as he looked around.

Matto motioned them forward into the deeper trees, weaving between trunks where the snow lay untouched. The air grew still, the silence stretching until every sound felt too loud.

The bitter scent thickened. Footsteps crunched in the snow, along with voices they didn't understand. Matto led them into a tight cluster of spruce, the needles brushing Brak's arms. Through the green shadows he saw them, two figures wrapped in thick coverings, each clutching a thunderstick.

The hairless ones slowed and stared at the snow. One knelt, a glove tracing the broad track, wide forefoot and splayed toes, the depth showing weight. The trail had betrayed them. Matto's frame tightened. Brak felt the heat of it and knew the anger was aimed at him, for the sign he had left.

The hairless ones followed the line toward the spruce. Brak's heart beat hard. Matto dropped lower and set an arm across Brak to hold him. The picture he sent was plain. *Stillness. Silence.*

The first figure came so close, Brak could see the hair around his mouth. The bitter tang of the thunderstick made Brak's nose twitch.

The second spoke quietly. The smell of fear came off them, raw and rank. They lingered, scanning the trees. Then both turned and followed their own tracks back. One glanced over a shoulder, eyes searching the shadows, but they did not return.

Only when their sounds had faded into the trees did Matto rise. His breath drifted in the cold as he checked the trail, then motioned for them to follow. No words passed between them.

Brak's heart was still pounding when they moved on. The unspoken truth was clear, they had been close enough to touch the hairless ones and yet gone unseen. It was a lesson Matto had given without speaking: patience and stillness could mean survival.

By the time night came, the wind had picked up. They found shelter in the shadow of a boulder, and Brak built his bedding as he had seen Kara do. She chattered lightly, sending him an image of woven branches and snow pressed into the gaps for warmth. Brak followed the example, pleased when the structure held. Matto gave no sign of approval, only settling himself with his back to the stone. Still, Brak kept glancing toward him in the fading light, hoping one day the larger male would see he was worth keeping close.

CHAPTER 5

The forest opened wider the next day, the trees spaced far enough apart that the morning light fell in long stripes across the snow. The air was still and cold enough to make each breath sting in Brak's nose. His legs ached, but the rhythm of moving had settled into him. He had started placing his steps more carefully, letting his weight down slowly the way Kara did.

He slowed and let the others draw a few paces ahead. *"Tired."*

Kara kept walking. She grunted, *"Keep going."*

He caught up, breath rough. *"Where we go?"*

Matto's eyes stayed forward. He grunted, *"Away."*

After a few steps: *"When stop?"*

"Not known yet."

Matto lengthened his stride, the talk done. Brak had to quicken to keep up.

By midday, Matto moved them toward a stand of pines where the snow lay deeper. He slowed, scanning ahead, then sent a brief image of the shape of something large moving through the white. Brak tried to see it but caught only flickers of shadow. Kara's ears twitched, her gaze narrowing.

Matto went forward, and Brak followed, though curiosity tugged at him. The shadows ahead thickened, and a scent came with them, warm and strong. It was not the bitter smell of thundersticks, but something heavy with life. He lagged, drawn toward it, and his eyes fixed on a massive shape parting the branches.

The hair along his shoulders lifted. A towering, long-legged creature stepped into view, its coat thick and brown, head held high. A smaller shape followed close at its side. Brak stared, caught between fascination and hunger. The calf's scent was rich and inviting, but the mother's presence made his skin tighten.

He took one step too many and the snow shifted with a faint hiss, the mother's head snapping toward him. For a heartbeat the world held still; she lowered her head, the hair along her neck lifting. Then she charged straight for him.

The ground shook under her hooves as she came with ears flat and nostrils flaring. Brak's chest clenched. Instinct drove him backward, but the speed of her charge forced him to turn and run. Snow burst up around his legs. Her grunts and the pounding of her steps chased him through the brush.

He spotted a tall spruce ahead and leapt for it, thick fingers finding purchase in the rough bark. He climbed fast, pulling himself up as her head struck the trunk. The wood shuddered beneath him. Brak clung there, panting, the mother staring up with dark, unblinking eyes.

Matto's heavy steps broke through the snow nearby. Kara appeared beside him, her gaze flicking from the moose to Brak. She gave a sharp chattering sound, almost like laughter, and Matto's eyes glinted, though he said nothing.

The mother moose hesitated, her calf calling from just inside the treeline. With one last glare toward Brak, she turned and trotted back to it. Brak climbed down slowly, his pride stinging more than his muscles.

Kara's amusement was open now, her teeth showing as she sent an image of him clinging to the tree like a frightened bear cub. Brak gave a low huff, but it lacked heat. Matto's only response was a glance toward the trail ahead before moving on, the faintest trace of amusement in his eyes.

Brak followed without a word, vowing to himself that the next time something charged at him, he would stand his ground.

CHAPTER 6

Hours without a halt had pared them thin. Steps shortened, bellies pulled hollow, thoughts slipping toward meat. Then the cover broke: light-barked trunks stood wide apart, giving to open ground scoured clean. Fences ran in straight lines. A long shed hunched beside a taller round bin. The air carried scents that did not belong to the woods: sweet, sharp, mineral.

Brak slowed, eyes narrowing at the strange shapes ahead. A tall cage of wood slats stood near the shed, packed to the ribs with yellow cobs that the wind rattled like teeth; beside it, a low heap of bright shapes lay frozen hard, round and orange and green, skins dulled by frost; near a stump, a pale block sat on a board, hoof marks in the snow around it where deer had licked.

Kara came to his side and tilted her head to breathe.

Smells curled into their noses and settled there, sweet from the frozen gourds, dusty from the dry kernels, bitter-bright from the salt.

She looked to Matto, half hidden by a trunk, broad and still, his gaze sweeping the yard and the square dwelling beyond the outbuildings. White breath plumed from a metal pipe on its roof. No voices carried, only the faint clink of something turning in the wind. He tested the air: hairless ones, stale, not today. His jaw tightened. They had not eaten. Hunger pulled at sense, yet the risk weighed more.

Brak took a half step forward and gave a quick, eager chatter.

He chattered, *"Food. Try."*

Matto's ears went back; for a long beat Brak thought the answer would be no, then the older male's jaw worked once and he grunted at last.

He grunted, *"Fast."*

Hunched over, they left the trees and crossed the open where wind had beaten the snow thin. The corn crib's smell grew strong and dusty, the frozen pumpkins gave off a sweet rot that teased the nose, and the salt block bit sharp at the back of the tongue even from a distance.

Kara went first to the pumpkin heap, chose one split by the freeze, and levered it open with a dull, hard crack; the inside shone glassy and cold, and she scooped a fist of flesh to chew slow, eyes narrowing as she weighed the value.

Matto walked to the crib, reached through the slats, caught a cob and snapped it free; kernels clacked under his thumb as he rubbed a strip clean and ate, the sound brittle and dry. He sent an image to Brak, simple and direct: *pull, strip, eat.*

Brak took his own cob, worked the yellow teeth loose, and bit; the taste came like sun held in stone and a low sound of approval rolled in his chest. He moved to the salt block, ran his tongue once along the edge, and the burn flooded his mouth; he licked again, then stopped himself and looked back to Matto.

Matto pointed with his chin toward the square dwelling and flared his nostrils.

He grunted, *"Watch."*

CHAPTER 7

Marcy Wiggins stood at the kitchen sink with warm water running over her hands. Beyond the window the back paddock lay flat and white, the shed and corn crib small against the snow. Steam fogged the glass; she cleared a circle with her wrist and watched for the deer that came to the salt. She kept scrubbing.

Something moved by the shed.

She paused, fingers slick with soap, and leaned closer. Even with her glasses on she had to squint to be sure. Three dark shapes slipped near the shed, too big for deer, too upright for bears. Her breath caught. She covered her mouth and took two small steps back from the window.

"Merv," she called over her shoulder, voice shaky. "Merv, come quick, and grab your gun."

In the next room, Merv sat in his recliner with the newspaper folded wide across his belly. He huffed, rustled the pages closed, and pushed himself up with a grunt.

"What is it now," he said, half to himself, shuffling into the kitchen. "Can a man finish a story in peace."

He came up behind her still grumbling, then followed the angle of her hand toward the back field. The shapes were clearer now, moving between the crib and the shed, thick through the shoulders, dark against the snow.

"What in God's name are those?" he said aloud.

Marcy did not answer. She stared through the glass without blinking.

Merv started mumbling as he crossed to the mudroom by the back door. He reached up to the wall rack, lifted the rifle from its hooks, and glanced once at Marcy before quietly opening the back door.

CHAPTER 8

The Sasquatch curved along the yard, taking what they could reach. Kara broke another gourd and set half near Brak, but he did not touch it again; the corn was better, and the salt pulled stronger.

The stillness split with a crack. Snow jumped at Brak's feet, and a splinter jerked from the board under the salt block while the hot scent of burned powder slid into the cold.

Matto's roar rolled across the yard, deep and fierce. Brak jolted and turned toward the source. A hairless one stood near the square dwelling with one foot braced in the snow and a thunderstick hard to its shoulder; smoke coiled from the stick's mouth while another hairless one moved at the door, throwing words they could not understand.

Matto chattered fast and clipped.

He grunted, *"Run. Now."*

The second crack came hard and close. Kara cried out, stumbled as one leg gave, and drove herself forward anyway; the smell of her blood snapped sharp in Brak's nose and he dropped the cob and ran. Another crack punched the shed and sent dry splinters into the air; corn in the crib rattled like rain.

Snow kicked up around their shins as they sprinted for the trees. Brak's breath came in hot bursts that steamed while his legs burned; he kept pace at Kara's side as she limped hard and Matto led them on.

At the treeline Matto pivoted, caught Kara under the arm, and hauled her through the first screen of spruce. They did not stop. They slipped deeper until the farm sounds thinned, then vanished, the wind weaving thicker among the trunks. Only then did Matto slow; he eased Kara into the lee of a fallen log, its hollow side turned from the farm, and Brak dropped to a knee beside her, chest heaving.

Matto bent to the wound. Blood had soaked the hair along her thigh and spilled in threads onto the snow; he gathered clean snow and packed it firm, then sent Brak a clear picture; *hands pressing above the hurt, firm and even.* Brak set both palms where Matto's mind put them and held, his weight set.

When the bleeding eased, Matto scraped moss from a nearby trunk and packed it into the cut, setting more snow around to cool the swell; his hands worked without waste while Brak watched the order of each move and kept his own where they were needed.

They listened. Farm sounds thinned back to wind and the faint clatter of the crib; no more cracks came and the hairless ones' voices were lost to distance and walls.

Kara lay with eyes half closed, breath steady but tight; when pain rose she set her teeth and rode it down. The day thinned toward gray. For a time the farm lay quiet behind them, then thin shouts rose on the wind and a metal clatter threaded the trees. Matto lifted his head and listened a long count, the sound coming and going as the wind swung. He touched Kara's shoulder and pointed downslope. He took one side and Brak the other, and together they moved, slow and careful, working along a shallow wash where water had cut the leaf mold, stepping in stone and water to hide their sign. The voices faded, the wind carried no trace of the farm, and still he kept them moving.

Near dusk they found a hollow under hemlock and dragged in boughs to break the wind. Matto slipped into the trees to hunt while Brak stayed with Kara, ears on distance and nose on wind. The forest settled to its old sounds, and now and then the faint rattle of corn moved far behind them.

When Matto returned he carried a small deer. They ate quick and quiet as fine snow began again. Brak lay close to Kara and listened for the small change in her breath that meant sleep had found her for a time, and he kept his eyes on the dark where the farm sat, a shape he could not see but could feel in the air, a sharp place in the wide cold.

****

By the second day, Brak's restlessness had grown too much to contain. When Matto prepared to leave to hunt again, Brak stepped in front of him and grunted with insistence. *"Take me."*

Matto studied him for a long moment, his expression unreadable. At last, he gave a short grunt of agreement.

****

The forest was hushed under a thin veil of falling snow. Brak followed closely, matching Matto's long stride as best he could. He watched how the older male placed his feet, how he shifted his weight to avoid sound, and how his eyes scanned constantly. Brak lowered his own steps, testing each patch of ground before putting his full weight down.

The forest was still, holding the scent of frost and old pine. Matto stopped, lifting his head slightly. Brak froze, tilting his ear toward the sound Matto had caught, the faint scrape of hooves breaking through snow, followed by a snort of warm breath. The scent followed, drifting to them in thin threads. Musk. Fur. Life.

Matto lowered himself, one arm out to signal Brak. *"Keep low."*

Brak bent forward, trying to still his breathing.

Through a tangle of spruce branches, a deer stood pawing at the snow for the grass beneath. Its ears flicked at the smallest sound. A wind came from the side, brushing over Matto's face, carrying their scent away from the prey. He studied the ground, marking the gap between them. There was no open path. He would have to drive it into the trees ahead.

Matto moved, each step careful. Brak followed, doing his best to mirror the older one's movements but kicking loose a clump of snow that tumbled down the slope. The deer's head shot up. Its eyes locked on them for a heartbeat before it bolted.

Matto burst forward, his legs driving through the snow with powerful strides. The deer crashed through a tangle of saplings, forcing Matto to push through branches that clawed at his face and shoulders. Brak tried to keep up but stumbled, his foot sinking deep. He wrenched it free and ran, the sound of the chase ringing in his ears, hooves pounding, snow spraying, Matto's deep breaths and the sharp crack of tree limbs breaking.

The deer veered toward a narrow run of open ground. Matto pushed harder, closing the gap with long, ground-eating steps. Brak swung wide, trying to flank it the way he had seen Kara do before. His heart pounded, his arms pumping. The deer turned again, back toward thicker trees, and Brak's movement cut off part of its path. It hesitated just long enough.

Matto slammed forward, wrapping his arms around the deer's neck. The weight and force drove both of them into the snow in a violent tangle. The deer thrashed, kicking hard enough to gouge the earth beneath the snow. Matto tightened his hold, his shoulder driving down against its chest until its struggles weakened. Then it stilled.

Matto stepped back and pointed at the deer. He grunted, *"You carry."*

Brak blinked in surprise but stepped forward, crouching to lift the body. His arms strained under the weight and he had to shift his footing to keep it balanced. Matto watched for a moment, then stepped in to adjust the deer over Brak's shoulder so the weight was more evenly spread. Brak took a breath, steadied himself, and began walking.

They headed back, the snow crunching softly underfoot. Brak's muscles burned with the effort, but he kept going. Halfway back, Matto reached out, took the deer from him without a word, and swung it up onto his own shoulder with ease. Brak followed, breathing hard but silently proud of himself and thankful to Matto for letting him help.

By the time they reached the shelter, Kara was already sitting up, waiting. Matto dropped the deer beside her, the soft snow beneath it melting from the heat of the body.

Brak stayed close to the deer, the pride still warm inside him.

CHAPTER 9

Kara tested her weight on her injured leg the next morning, leaning forward until her foot pressed into the snow. A soft grunt left her, but she did not pull back. She took another slow step, then another, her breath steady. Matto watched without speaking, his eyes narrowing in quiet assessment. When she straightened and gave a short nod, he turned away, leading them deeper into the forest.

The snow began lightly, drifting down in small, quiet flakes that clung to their hair. Brak tilted his head up, catching a few on his face before brushing them away. The light flurry became thicker, the flakes growing heavy and fast. Soon the forest floor was hidden under a fresh layer. The trees blurred together in the whiteness.

By midday the world was a white wall in motion. Brak could barely see Kara ahead of him. The wind rose to a howl and drove needles of cold at his face. Snow whipped into his eyes and he blinked hard to clear it. Kara hunched forward, her hair rimed with ice, each step a slow push through deepening drifts.

Matto did not slow. His shape moved ahead, dark against the swirl, and whenever the wind eased Brak caught him scanning the land and angling their line. The snow was knee-deep in places and Brak's legs ached from forcing a path.

The blizzard thickened until the world shrank to a few arm-lengths. Their double coats worked, dense underhair holding heat while guard hairs shed the worst of the fall, yet the chill still found seams and settled on skin like icy stones. Brak's chest tightened with unease; he had never known snow to come this heavy.

Matto angled them toward higher ground, guiding them along the edge of a ridge until massive boulders loomed ahead, dark and solid against the white. He strode to the largest pair, crouched, and began clawing at the snow between them. His hands worked quickly, tearing away frozen layers until the rock beneath showed through. Ice cracked under his weight. Brak and Kara stood side by side, watching him carve out a hollow deep enough to crouch inside.

Matto glanced back at them, then motioned to quickly. get in.

Kara limped forward first, lowering herself into the hollow. Brak followed, curling his body against hers for warmth. The boulders blocked part of the wind, but snow still swirled down from above. Matto stepped into the gap, his broad back to the storm, and began pulling snow in behind them, packing it to close them in. The light dimmed until only a faint glow seeped through cracks in the snow.

The wind roared outside, battering against Matto's back. The cold no longer cut at Brak as deeply. His breathing slowed. He could hear Kara's stable breaths beside him and the low, constant rumble of the storm beating at their shelter. Matto's bulk was a wall of heat against the worst of it.

Brak rested his head against Kara, thinking of the way his mother used to curl herself around him and his sister in the colder nights. The memory was soft, her chest rising against his face and the small sounds she made in sleep.

Brak's eyes drifted shut, and for the first time in days, he slept without the bite of cold at his back.

CHAPTER 10

After just over two months on the move, through blizzards and thin meat, skirting hairless ones and taking what the land gave, they came into new land the hairless ones call South Dakota. Snow pooled along the sheltered sides of the rocks and filled the hollows. They crossed a frozen creek and climbed to a rise where great boulders stood like ribs. Beyond, the ground fell away in a long drop into shadow.

Brak's gaze drifted to the horizon, where a dull line of trees blurred into the gray sky. The land felt different here. The hills rolled in a way the forest back home never had, and the wind spoke a harsher language. He felt smaller here yet exposed.

They moved slowly over the uneven ridge. The snow here was crusted on top, breaking underfoot in irregular patches that echoed faintly in the stillness. Kara stayed a few paces ahead. Matto moved behind Brak, his broad frame shadowing him, scanning the rocks and shadows with a steady, unblinking gaze.

At first Brak noticed only the normal scents of winter stone and dry pine, but then a faint bitterness began to thread through them. It was distant enough to dismiss, yet it clung in his nostrils in a way that made him uneasy. He lifted his chin and breathed in again, catching the trace more clearly this time.

The wind shifted, and the scent thickened. Musky, sour, alive. Matto lifted his head and drank it in, jaw setting. Kara angled her face to the breeze, eyes narrowing. They knew the stink. Brak watched them and felt his own pace slow.

They passed between two leaning boulders that made a narrow throat in the ridge. Snow here was broken not by the loose scuff of deer but by heavier, cautious steps. Matto crouched and set his palm beside a print, the edges ragged from wind yet deep, the pads clear, a long drag scoring forward. Kara's shoulders tightened. She touched another mark with two fingers and looked up-slope.

A light flurry slid in from the west, dusting their hair and softening the churned snow as wind moved through the rock gaps like a slow breath. Matto opened his hand once, a small clear signal, and Brak pressed close to the stones.

The climb steepened, and the rocks shouldered closer until they had to go single file. Somewhere above a lone bird called once and went still.

Snow answered under a careful step ahead. They froze. Kara's head turned a fraction. Matto leaned into the gap between stones and peered.

The sound came again, closer, slow and sure. Brak lowered his body, ready to spring if Matto moved, and the three of them waited.

Silence stretched until the air felt heavy. A shadow flickered between two boulders. Snow sloughed from an overhang with a faint hiss, and a sudden blur broke cover.

A snow hare burst across the ridge, its body low and quick. Brak flinched toward Kara before he knew it for what it was. The animal kicked powder and vanished into a drift without a sound.

He let a breath go. Kara's mouth twitched once. Matto's gaze stayed on the drift as if weighing whether the false rush had teeth behind it. He motioned them on.

The wind turned again, and the stink hit harder, thick enough to taste. Matto's ears tipped forward. Kara bared her teeth a sliver. This was no prey. This was a hunter.

Steps came, heavy and placed, pressing deep. A scrape of claw on stone carried down the cut.

A tall shape slid between the rocks, hair matted at the legs where snow had clung, movement smooth and full of intent. They called it a Kreth. The hairless ones would name it Dogman. Its eyes found them and the ridge narrowed to that single line of sight.

The Kreth came fast, weaving through stone in long, fluid strides. Breath steamed from its mouth, jaw parting to show wet teeth. Brak planted his feet, but the hit still drove him back, claws raking his arm. He shoved upward to break its balance; it was stronger than he had guessed. Jaws snapped, as it caught a tuft of his hair, and tore it free.

They hit the snow and rolled. The edge of the drop felt too close. Claws bit into his shoulder and he roared, twisting hard and flinging the thing off. It landed light, chest working, and came again.

This time Brak met it head-on, arms locking around its torso. They stumbled in a violent push and pull, their feet digging deep into the snow as they fought for ground. The Kreth tried to hook a leg around his and throw him, but Brak lowered his center and shoved forward, driving them toward a patch of jagged rock.

The beast twisted suddenly, tearing free and circling to his side. Before Brak could turn fully, claws raked across his ribs. Pain flashed white in his mind. The Kreth seized the moment to leap, bearing him to the ground again. Teeth snapped close enough for him to feel the spray of hot breath across his face.

Brak slammed his elbow into its neck, rolled, and planted both feet into its midsection. He heaved with all his strength, sending it skidding back. The Kreth rose immediately, shaking snow from its fur, a deep growl vibrating through its chest.

Matto's roar cut through the wind, a deep, shuddering sound that seemed to fill the ridge. He closed the distance in three strides, striking the Kreth in the side with bone-jarring force. The impact sent both of them tumbling into the snow.

The Kreth slashed wildly, claws catching Matto's forearm, but Matto bore down, gripping its shoulders and driving it onto its back. The creature twisted, trying to bring its jaws to his throat, but Matto shifted his weight, pinning it harder. He wrenched it upward, spun once, and hurled it toward the edge.

The beast landed hard, scrabbling at the icy ground. Matto charged again, slammed into its chest, and sent it tumbling over the ridge. The Kreth vanished from sight, a fading thud echoing from far below.

Brak stayed on one knee for a moment, chest heaving. Kara had not hidden, her body angled toward them, ready to step in if needed. She met Brak's eyes briefly, assessing the blood on his shoulder and ribs before looking at Matto.

Matto scanned the drop for a few breaths longer, then turned back toward them. He did not speak, but somewhere deep inside a faint and unfamiliar feeling stirred. It was a small flicker of protectiveness toward Brak, one he had not expected and could not quite ignore.

They stayed a short time, listening to the wind scour the ridge. Brak wiped blood from his arm. Kara packed his cuts with ice from a shaded drift. The sting dulled, and another feeling rose. He almost asked why they had not stepped in sooner. The question reached his tongue and stopped. He saw Kara watching and caught the way Matto's eyes weighed him. The answer was there. They had wanted to see if he could stand on his own.

When Matto moved past him, Brak followed without a word, his steps quicker than before. Kara glanced at them both, eyes narrowing as if she sensed the shift between them. Matto's gait stayed steady, but Brak noticed the small angle of his head, the way he kept him within view. Storm clouds deepened, and the light grew dim, yet Brak felt a little less exposed than before. The quiet, unspoken change between them held like a shield as they left the ridge behind.

CHAPTER 11

The wind pushed against them as they moved west, its cold bite cutting through the thick hair on their backs. The trees had thinned over the last day, replaced by long stretches of open ground where cover was scarce. The air here smelled older, sharper, carrying traces of distant animals and faint hints of the hairless ones that had passed through recently.

Brak's steps had slowed. His breathing came heavier now, each stride seeming to drag him farther from his strength. Kara moved ahead, nose to the wind, checking sign and choosing the firmest ground. Matto kept his pace unbroken, eyes forward, scanning for the next rise, the next patch of cover, the next place worth resting.

After a time Brak chattered softly, catching up just enough to speak. He grunted, *"Why stop not here? Trees. Water close."*

Matto's head turned slightly, but he kept walking. He chattered, *"Still too close to home. They follow our scent. Must not make it worth it for them."*

Brak's brow furrowed. He replied, *"We walk many suns. They give up."*

Matto slowed only enough to look back at him, chattering, *"The strong do not give up. They remember. They wait. We keep moving until they will not follow."*

Kara glanced over her shoulder, her expression unreadable, but Brak caught the faintest flicker in her gaze. A quiet acceptance, as if she had heard such warnings before and had learned not to argue.

The ground underfoot shifted from frozen soil to a thin crust of ice. It cracked softly with each step, a sound too loud in the emptiness. Brak's shoulders tensed as he realized how far their noise might carry. Matto seemed to notice it too, leading them toward a cluster of dark rocks that jutted up like broken teeth from the earth.

They moved between the stones, where the wind's howl was muted. Brak kept glancing over his shoulder, certain he could hear something beyond the gusts. Each time he looked, the land stretched back empty, the horizon bending away under the pale winter sun.

Matto finally stopped beneath a low ridge and signaled for them to rest in the shallow shelter between two boulders. Brak sank down with relief, legs aching, chest rising and falling in slow pulls of air.

Somewhere in the distance, a single sound broke the stillness. It was faint, too faint to place, but carried the shape of movement that was not the wind. Brak's ears turned toward it, but when he looked to Matto, the older one had already shifted his weight and was staring out over the land, listening.

Matto said nothing. He only stood there for a long moment, his gaze fixed on the horizon, before finally stepping back into the shadow of the rocks.

CHAPTER 12

The ridge thinned until the world felt like a spine of stone under their feet, wind pouring along it and curling snow into ribbons that broke and flew. One side fell away into trees and ice; the other rose steep into broken slabs. Their path wound between, just wide enough for one.

They rounded a bend and stopped. A boulder had slumped from the slope and jammed tight against the outer edge, wind-packed snow locking it in place. No room to slip by. The drop beyond swallowed sound.

Matto measured ledges and cracks. Kara read the stone quick, crouched under the lower lip, glanced along the brittle shelf above, and the small buried rocks at its base like teeth.

She grunted, *"We move it."*

Matto chattered, *"Too heavy. Slope bad. Drop worse."*

Kara scraped the uphill side to dark rock and pointed Brak to loose stones. He brought them with numb fingers. She wedged the first, then the next, setting teeth under the boulder while Matto watched.

"Push slow," Kara said. *"When it moves, hold."*

They leaned. The rock resisted, then gave a breath. Snow cracked. Kara drove another wedge. Another breath. Wind clawed their backs. Far below a tree creaked once.

Brak's feet slipped; he caught himself against the stone. *"Set feet,"* Kara said. *"Push with legs."*

The boulder yielded a finger's width and stuck.

Kara looked at the shelf and chose. *"Break white skin. Not all. Wet rock. Then push."*

Matto nicked the crust in small scoops until the face slicked, slid back to place, and set his weight. Kara nodded. They pressed. Wet stone turned force to glide. The boulder rolled and opened a narrow mouth between its edge and the drop.

Kara grunted, "Stop."

Kara tested first, side-on, spine to cold rock, and slipped through. Brak set himself as she had and began to slide. Halfway his heel met nothing and his body tilted. Matto pinned the boulder with one forearm, caught the hair at the back of Brak's shoulder, and drew him in until heel found stone again. Brak did not look down. He slid through.

Kara looked to Matto and chattered, *"Your turn. I hold."*

He braced a palm, kept his weight in his legs, and edged across with the same quiet force he carried into a fight. Then he stood with them.

They did not celebrate. The wind did it, a thin keen along the ridge. Kara walked a few paces and looked back. The boulder sat crooked in its nest. The path was open.

Brak touched the back of his fist to his chest, to the stone, then to her forearm. He grunted, *"Strong."*

Kara's mouth twitched as she chattered, *"Push right place. Not only hard."*

Matto listened to what the wind carried and what it did not. He grunted, *"Move."*

They went single file along the opened path, Kara testing each step, Brak copying their angles, Matto behind watching the line and the sky.

Beyond the bend the ridge widened to a saddle where snow lay unmarked. Wind eased. They paused in the lee of twisted pines without sitting, legs loose, hearts slowing.

Brak glanced back; Kara touched his shoulder and he steadied. Matto met Kara's eyes for a breath. She dipped her head a fraction in return. Not thanks. Not asking. An exchange that said she would do it again if the land asked.

A flurry slid across the ground and moved on. In its wake a thin scent arrived that belonged to neither rock nor snow nor pine. Kara turned first. Brak caught it a moment later.

Matto grunted, *"Go."*

They moved on, the pass behind them, the scent unwelcome but far, their bodies falling into the tight shape of a small, hard band that had pushed a mountain aside and kept walking.

CHAPTER 13

The trees thinned until the ground ahead opened into a strange, pale strip that cut through the land. It was wide and flat, sealed under a hard dark skin that smelled bitter and odd. The air carried a faint taint of hairless ones and metal, an unnatural smell against snow and cottonwoods. Brak slowed, eyeing the distance across. His chest lifted in an uneasy breath. He knew the hairless ones' machines moved fast along these open paths, far faster than even a Sasquatch.

Matto chattered, *"Move before a hairless one comes."*

Brak's feet stayed where they were for a moment too long. Kara stepped forward, her eyes fixed ahead, ready to cross. Hunger tugged at all three of them, a dull ache that made patience harder to find.

Brak finally moved, his stride quickening to follow Kara.

Matto led, his mind already on the shelter of the next tree line.

A low growl of sound rose from beyond the rise to their right. Matto's ears twitched. The sound deepened, growing louder with startling speed. Over the crest of the rise came the machine, its eyes bright and glaring. The smell of heat, smoke, and hairless one clung to it. It bore down fast, far too fast.

Brak froze mid-stride.

Matto grunted, *"Move!"*, but the warning came too late.

The machine swerved hard, its scream of noise cutting across the still air. Its thick black rings gripped and slid against the ground, leaving black smears on the hard skin. It lurched sideways, one side lifting slightly before slamming down. It skidded, metal shrieking, then jolted into a ditch with a bone-jarring crash. The air burst with the acrid scent of burned stone and twisted metal.

Brak stumbled back from the edge of the strip, his breath fast. Kara's gaze shot toward the wreckage. The machine had stilled, its front twisted and smoking faintly. Inside, the hairless one slumped forward, unmoving.

Matto huffed in annoyance. He turned away and kept

walking.

Kara chattered sharply, *"Help them."* Her voice carried the weight of command. Brak shook, glancing between her and Matto.

Matto did not slow.

Kara moved first, crossing the remaining distance with powerful strides. Brak followed, still rattled by how close the machine had come. They reached the dented side and pulled at the frame, metal groaning under their grip. Kara braced her weight, using both arms to wrench the door wide enough for Brak to reach in.

The hairless one's chest rose and fell in slow breaths. Their scent carried fear, sweat, and the coppery smell of blood. Brak pulled them out, the limp weight awkward in his arms, and lowered them to the ground beside the wreck.

Kara knelt briefly, studying the rise and fall of their chest before stepping back. She looked toward Matto, her expression tight.

Matto stood farther down the strip, waiting in the shadow of the trees.

They left the hairless one near the machine, knowing the

others of its kind would come. Without another glance back, Kara and Brak crossed to the other side where Matto waited. His face was set, eyes hard.

He turned and walked ahead of them, his pace faster than before. Hunger gnawed at his patience, and Brak's hesitation still burned in his mind. He wanted nothing to do with hairless ones, not their noise, not their machines, not their scent. And he wanted Brak to understand that paying attention was the only thing keeping them alive.

CHAPTER 14

After walking for two days without a proper rest, Matto had found a safe rock overhang, and Brak, for once, let himself enjoy the rest. The ground was hard, but the shelter kept the wind off them and held some of their heat at night. Twenty feet ahead, the treeline marked the start of a steep drop into a valley. At night the stars spread across the sky in a pale river of light.

Matto never said why they stayed, and neither Kara nor Brak asked. As the sun went down, he left to hunt alone. He returned with food but offered only a grunt before lying down with his back turned. Kara felt the tension in every movement, as if he held something inside that might break if pushed. Brak kept close to her and gave him space.

They sat on two flat boulders near the edge of the overhang, looking at the stars. The valley stretched wide below, the trees swaying in the faint wind.

Brak chattered, breaking the quiet, *"Kara… you show me? Throw stones. Kill food?"*

Kara grunted, *"Yes."*

Brak picked at a scab on his forearm and looked over the valley. He grunted, *"I want to be strong."*

Kara watched the dark. *"You will."*

Brak chattered, *"I miss the old place. I miss my mother and the little one. I miss the others."*

Kara kept her eyes on the trees. *"The old place is gone. You cannot go back."*

Silence held. He looked at her and chattered, *"Why does he not like me?"*

Kara did not turn. She replied, *"Matto carries much. Not just wounds on the outside."*

The stillness between them was broken by a faint crack. Both of their heads turned. Somewhere in the treeline, a twig had snapped.

They caught the scent in the same breath. Sasquatch.

Male. Alone.

Kara's lips peeled back from her teeth in a low growl.

Brak followed, his own growl rumbling in his chest.

The air carried the male's scent, strong and sharp. He moved with intent, keeping just out of sight as he watched them from the brush. They tracked the sound of his steps in the shifting shadows.

The forest fell silent.

Then he came from the dark. Taller than Kara but on the slim side, his body was all corded muscle. He moved with a sudden burst of speed, eating the distance in two long strides, arms spread as if to seize Brak by the neck.

Kara was already moving. She threw herself at him, the collision cracking like a branch breaking. Her shoulder slammed his ribs hard enough to jar her own bones and sent them both staggering into the undergrowth, dirt and dry leaves flying.

As they grappled, Brak threw his head back and let loose a high, tearing call, half scream and half roar, a summons for Matto hunting downridge.

The male recovered first. He twisted and swung, nails flashing in the dim. They raked across Kara's side, opening hot, burning lines. She snarled and drove her forearm into his face, bone on bone. He grunted but did not yield, locking one arm around her and trying to drag her down.

She slammed her knee up into his stomach, once, twice, until his grip loosened. She lunged for his throat, fingers closing on the thick muscle there, but he crashed his forehead into hers and stars burst across her sight. He shoved her back and came again, nails catching her arm and twisting it.

Kara's roar tore through the trees.

Brak launched himself at the male's back, arms locking around his neck, legs kicking to drag him off her. The male reached behind without looking, grabbed Brak by the shoulder, and hurled him sideways. Brak hit a tree with a hollow thud and slid to the ground.

Kara's focus flicked toward Brak for an instant, and that was enough for the male to slam her to the ground. Her back struck hard, knocking the breath from her chest. He bore down, one hand closing over her throat, the other pressing her head toward the dirt. She clawed at his forearm, kicking wildly, but his weight held her.

He hauled her head up and drove it toward the earth again.

Matto appeared in a blur. His fist crashed into the side of the male's skull with the force of a boulder rolling downhill, the crack ringing through the trees. The male dropped at once, sprawling in the needles.

Matto was on him before he could turn. His fists rose and fell in a brutal rhythm, each strike thudding into bone and muscle. The male thrashed, swinging wild, but Matto's blows came faster, heavier. He smashed the jaw with a hook, then drove his forehead down into the stunned face.

The male tried to grab at Matto's arm, to twist free, but Matto wrenched his arm loose and drove his elbow into the male's temple. A wet sound followed, and the male's body jerked.

Matto kept going. He hammered the side of the skull, then the bridge of the nose, breaking cartilage and sending blood across his knuckles. The male's legs kicked in the dirt, slower now, weaker.

Even when the male stopped fighting, Matto did not relent. His fists rose and fell, smashing until the body beneath him sagged into stillness.

At last, he pulled back, breath ragged, hands and forearms dripping with blood. His gaze was locked on the ruin in front of him, his chest heaving with each inhale.

Kara pushed herself to her knees, her head throbbing, her side burning from the gashes, and her arm aching where it had been twisted. Brak was already crawling toward her, still dazed.

The stars above were still and distant, but all around them the night air clung heavy with the scent of blood and violence.

Matto stayed where he was, shoulders lifting and settling, heavy breaths ghosting in the cold.

CHAPTER 15

Blood clung to Matto hair, warm in some places, already drying in others. He leaned back, wiped his forearm across his mouth, and spat.

Without a word he rose, stepped over the corpse, and went into the trees. He followed his churned tracks to where he had dropped the deer when the fight began, slung it across his shoulder, and came back. The head lolled against his back then he dropped it near the overhang. The thud was dull.

Matto grunted, *"Eat. Then we move."*

He jerked his chin toward the dead male sprawled in the dirt. *"Others come. When he not return."*

Kara's chest still heaved from the fight, her arms trembling as she stood and stepped toward the deer. Her gaze flicked to the body and back, unease passing through her eyes. She knew Matto was right.

Brak stood looking into the dark treeline.

He grunted, barely loud enough to be heard. *"Others... come fast?"*

Matto only looked at him, then bent to tear into the deer's hide with his teeth, skin ripping away in coarse strands. Kara joined him, her fingers pulling strips free. Brak hesitated before moving closer, crouching and eating in silence.

When they had their fill, Matto rose and slung the deer over his shoulder again. He glanced at the dead male once more, then turned toward the shadows of the forest.

"We go," he grunted. *"To river."*

Brak followed behind Kara, his head turning to look at the dead male one last time. Worry lingered in his eyes, but he said nothing.

The three of them slipped into the trees, the darkness swallowing them as they moved, their steps quick and quiet. The sound of the river was far ahead, faint but constant, pulling them deeper into the night.

CHAPTER 16

The trees parted to reveal water that should have been a slow winter snake but was not. The river was swollen and pinched tight by rock, its middle a white throat where the current tore. Somewhere upstream a thaw or a broken jam had let go. Foam ripped past, and the sound filled the night like a thing that did not care who stepped into it.

Matto stopped on the bank, shoulders lifted, head tilted to weigh the far side. Spray tasted like stone. He dropped the deer from his shoulder, scanned the dark line of trees across, then lifted the carcass again. He grunted, *"In. Lose scent."*

Brak watched the surge and boil around hidden teeth. He grunted, *"Cold."*

Matto did not look at him. He chattered, *"Cold better than being found. Cross fast. Stay low. Hold each other if you slip."*

Kara stepped first. Water took her to the knee and shoved. She widened, pushed back. Matto slid in beside her, the river to his thighs, the pull biting like many hands. Brak followed, teeth set, breath short as the chill climbed to his hips.

They moved as a line, angled a little upstream so the flow would not throw them too far between steps. The roar thickened near the throat. Stones rolled under Matto, slick as peeled bark. He kept low, arms loose, eyes hunting the next hold.

The river was not only fast. It was angry. It slammed them hard enough to steal air. Kara bent and leaned into it. Brak copied her shape, but his smaller body took the shocks deeper. The cold burned into joints. Fingers went blunt. Breath came in hard pulls.

A black swell struck from the side. Brak lost his footing and dropped. The river swallowed him. Kara caught a fistful of his hair and hauled. He coughed once and clung to her forearm.

Matto shouldered into the strongest line to take the force first. He reached for Kara's free wrist and pulled them close, setting their bodies into one tight shape the current could hit without breaking.

Another surge rose, taller. It struck and spun the deer on Matto's shoulder, then clawed what he carried. The river found the carcass, yanked, and turned the weight into a drag. The pull tore him off balance. He tried to keep both the meat and the line with Kara and Brak, but the current wrenched the carcass sideways like a hooked fish. Hide slid through his grip, rolled once in the boil, and vanished into the black throat around a jut of stone.

Matto's jaw locked. He did not reach after it. A low growl rose at the loss, meat scarce and hard won.

They pushed deeper. The throat hammered their legs and hips, trying to spin and bend them under. The cold ate at strength. Brak's calves cramped; he forced his feet open and stamped to keep blood moving. Kara's hands were numb on Brak's arm, but her grip held.

Matto angled them to a midstream rock that rose like a wet shoulder. He threw weight into the water, let it shove him sideways, caught the stone with his palm, and leaned. Pressure eased for a breath behind him. He swept the far bank with his eyes. The line through the next waves was narrow, but it would do.

He chattered over the roar, *"Go. One at a time. I hold."*

Kara shook her head once and grunted, *"Brak first."*

Matto set harder against the rock, made a wall with his body. Brak edged around, feet searching bottom he could not feel. A curl of water hit his ribs and flipped him. His hands shot out. One found Matto's forearm, the other slick stone. Matto's arm went rigid. He hauled Brak in and shoved him up onto the flat of the shoulder.

Brak sprawled, chest heaving, water pouring off him. He slapped thighs and calves with open palms to wake them. Kara slid along the edge behind him, letting her hip drag to slow. Matto followed last, back to the current, palms down to keep them from being peeled off.

The rock gave them three breaths. No more. Ahead the throat narrowed again, then fanned. Hit the fan wrong and it would dump them into a blind whirl that did not give bodies back quickly.

He grunted, *"Move."*

They slid off the far side together. The cold hit deeper. The river rose to Kara's chest, to Matto's waist, to Brak's mouth. Brak lifted his chin above the chop. Kara braced him with her shoulder. The bottom lifted and dropped. Matto reached over both, planted his heel on solid stone, and dragged forward a half step, then another.

The pinch wanted to turn them. Matto let it turn him instead, pivoting so the blow took his back, not his chest. He set a palm to Kara's back to keep her square and held his other hand near Brak's shoulder to clamp down if the river tried to take him again.

They moved by inches. Water clawed and tore. A hidden log bore down, its end lifting like a head. Matto saw the shadow and shoved Brak down by the neck. The log scraped his spine and smashed Kara's shoulder, twisting her. She snarled, shoved it off, and dug for bottom until she found it.

The far bank drew closer. The force spread. Matto shifted his angle and drove his foot onto a bed of smaller stones that did not roll. One long step, then another, the pull creeping from ribs to waist to thighs.

Brak's foot wedged on a ridge. He grunted hard when pain shot through his calf. The current pinned him. Kara looped an arm across his chest and leaned to hold him up while Matto reached, found his ankle, twisted and lifted, freed the foot, and shoved him into slacker water.

They stumbled the last body length together. Brak half crawled up the icy muddy slope, knees sinking, hands clawing for grass. Kara followed, each breath a stab from cold. Matto came last and did not stop until he stood above them on hard ground, chest working in slow, controlled breaths.

They shook, all three. Water streamed from hair and limbs. Night wind found every wet place and bit. Brak's teeth rattled. He slapped arms and legs harder, as if he could beat the cold out.

Matto grunted, *"Run."*

Brak panted once. He grunted, *"Why."*

Matto grunted, *"Get warm."*

They ran the forest at a steady pace, weaving the open lines between trunks, lifting knees through brush. At first the cold burned and their limbs felt made of stone, but soon heat climbed the big muscles and a little steam lifted from their skin. Breath found a rhythm. Snow hissed underfoot.

An hour later Matto grunted, *"Stop."*

He pointed to a wall of heavy brush, willow and cedar knitted tight, a pocket that would break most of the wind.

Brak chattered, *"I am hungry again."*

Matto responded, *"No food now. Later."* He tapped the

opening and pointed. *"Kara go."*

Kara crawled in and curled her back to the wind side. Brak followed, turning so his chest met her spine. Matto slid in last and sealed the gap with his weight. They huddled close, heat pooling where bodies met, and listened to the far forest sounds: branch creak, a distant owl, the faint run of water, until fatigue took them.

CHAPTER 17

Matto woke at once and drew scent. The cold bit deep into his nostrils, but beneath the winter smell of spruce and frozen soil came the bitter stink that did not belong to the woods.

Hairless ones. He sat up slowly, his massive frame shifting against the hard ground. Kara stirred beside him, opening one eye, then pushing herself up as the scent reached her too. Brak lifted his head and grunted low in question. Matto's reply was a short growl that silenced him.

They stayed crouched in the thicket, the dense tangle of branches hiding them from sight. The air was still. No wind to carry their own scent away. It would be easy to stay unnoticed, but the smell of the hairless ones grew stronger until their shapes moved between the trees, stepping closer. They were not on a game trail, only wandering through the woods, perhaps following the tracks of some smaller prey. In their hands gleamed thundersticks.

The three Sasquatch grunted softly to each other in short bursts.

Kara chattered a warning, *"No harm."*

Matto's muscles tightened. His instinct screamed to hurt them, especially at the sight of the thundersticks, the dangerous tools that had felled so many of his kind. He stayed still as the male hairless ones drew closer, until they were nearly upon him.

With a sudden surge, Matto pushed through the branches, snow shaking from his shoulders. He rose to his full height and let a deep growl build until it broke into a roar that rolled through the trees. The hairless ones jolted as if struck. One's mouth opened without sound, eyes wide and white, knees buckling until he dropped his thunderstick into the snow. The other tried to lift theirs but the barrel shook and dipped. Skin went gray. Breath came short and fast. A hot reek of urine cut the cold as dark spread down a pant leg. Both staggered back, hands up without meaning to raise them. Matto's eyes flicked once to the side, catching Brak standing straight now, worry etched on his young face, and Kara close beside him.

He turned back to the hairless ones, stooped, and lifted the fallen thunderstick from the snow. It snapped in his hands with a sharp screech. Then he took the other from the unsteady grip and bent it double. He hurled both twisted sticks into the drifts and moved past them without a backward glance. Relief slid through Kara and Brak, glad he had not harmed the hairless ones. They went with him into the trees, leaving the hairless ones rooted where they stood, silent and trembling, trying to make sense of what they had just seen.

CHAPTER 18

They were not on a trail. That was the first thing Lyle knew after twenty minutes of pushing through tight young firs, the boughs whispering against his jacket. The snow was ankle deep and old, crusted with a skin that sometimes held and sometimes gave with a brittle pop. Their breath smoked in front of them. The cold made every sound too clean.

"We're off the section line," Hank said. "Should've cut east a ways back."

"We ain't lost," Lyle told him. "Creek's ahead. Hit that and we're right."

"Feels off."

"Quit jawin'. You're gonna scare off every critter for a mile."

"Rabbit crossed here," Hank said a few paces later. He bent and slid a gloved finger along two neat ovals pressed into the crust. "Fresh enough."

Lyle nodded and shifted the rifle on his shoulder. Somewhere behind them a single magpie called twice and went quiet, like the woods had put a hand over its mouth.

They moved again, stepping around low blowdowns, easing past brush that snagged at cloth. The light was the dead gray that lives under unbroken cloud. Lyle glanced back once, out of habit, checking the faint line of their prints.

The smell found them first. It did not drift; it hit. Rank and sour, a sweet-rotten backnote, ammonia and copper, wet hair left in a warm room. It slid down the throat and turned the stomach. Lyle flinched.

"You smell that?" he whispered.

Hank gave one slow nod. He did not like it.

They listened. The world held still. No wind. The cold knitted itself between the branches so tight that even the small sounds of their bodies seemed too loud. Lyle heard his own pulse. He shifted a boot and the crust made a dry crack.

Something moved inside the thicket ahead. Not enough

to see. Hank turned his head a fraction. Lyle tightened his grip and felt the fine shake that came from cold or nerves, he could not tell which.

"Bear?" he mouthed.

Hank's eyes said no.

The brush was dense. It should have made anything crawl. Instead, the branches parted under a slow, steady shove; snow fell in sheets from the needles, and a shape rose from the thicket unlike anything they had ever seen.

Lyle's mind went empty for a heartbeat.

It was tall. Taller than any man he had ever stood near, shoulders like a slab, its hair, not fur, was long and dark. A rough ruff stood around the neck where snow had caught and clung. It straightened and kept straightening until the crown brushed low limbs and sent a soft patter of ice down.

Its face was not a mask. Eyes set deep under a heavy ridge. A wide, flat nose. The mouth opened and kept opening, wider than Lyle thought a mouth could go, black tongue showing, teeth big and blunt like a horse's and too many of them. It looked at them. Not past them. At them.

"Holy shiiit," Hank breathed, long and thin.

The sound that came did not start loud. It built. A deep roll rising from somewhere behind the ribs to the throat until it became a full roar that shook in Lyle's chest and made his knees soften. It felt like standing next to a jet engine. Both men clapped hands over their ears and shied from the noise without moving their feet. Heat spread sudden down Lyle's leg and he knew it was him. Shame and fear came up together and neither would stop.

Lyle tried to speak. "Back... up," he got out, thin and shaky.

Hank started to lift his rifle, then stopped, eyes flicking to the small .22 stamped on the barrel. A squirrel gun. It would do nothing to this behemoth. The front bead wobbled and he let the barrel drift low.

The tall one stepped forward. It never broke eye contact. Then its gaze shifted to its own side and back into the brush behind, where a smaller shape watched; it held there for a breath before returning to the men. The look that came back was flat and hard. It looked pissed.

Lyle's fingers forgot what to do. His rifle slipped and thumped into the snow. The tall one stooped without hurry and lifted it by the barrel. Thick fingers closed, the stock creaked, and metal cried as the barrel bent. The sound was thin and wrong in the trees. The rifle twisted into an S.

Hank still held his. The tall one reached, not fast. Hank could have pulled the trigger ten times before that hand arrived if this had been any normal fear. He did not pull it at all. He gave the rifle like a boy hands over a tool when his father says enough. The tall one bent that one too, steel and walnut complaining, and flung both ruined pieces into the drift without looking.

Up close Lyle saw scars crossing the hair along its face and ribs. The stink of it was den and musk and copper. Behind it, two more shapes held the thicket. The smaller one set a little back, worry in the set of the eyes even with all that hair. The other was female, wide in the shoulders and still as a stump, her gaze dark and unreadable. For a second Lyle thought: family.

"Do… do we run?" Hank whispered, as if even the thought might offend.

Lyle did not answer. He did not know if running would make them prey. He did not know if not running already had.

The tall one turned away first. It stepped past them, close enough Lyle felt the air move, and walked in a line between trunks with a steadiness that belonged to this place. The two behind followed. They did not look back. There was no crouch, no baring of teeth. They moved as if this had been a talk and it was finished.

Lyle shook without meaning to. The cold rushed back into his fingers like a pain waking up. Hank set a hand on his shoulder and found it was shaking too. The snow held the marks where the thing had stood. Not man. Not bear. Wide forefoot. Splayed toes. Sunk deep.

"What in God's name was that?" Hank asked.

Lyle walked over to it without thinking and reached for the twisted ruin. He stopped before his glove touched it, as if the metal might burn. The bend was obscene, like an arm turned the wrong way. He looked into the thicket and saw nothing now but the winter dark.

They waited until the sounds came back to the forest one by one. A creak from a loaded tree. A single raven, far off. The soft hiss of flakes falling from a limb. Lyle swallowed and tasted bile and the ghost of that bitter scent.

"Let's get the fuck outta here," he said.

They backed out the way they had come, placing their feet in their own prints because it felt like the only right thing left. Hank kept cutting his eyes to the sides. Lyle kept his on the ground because looking up made his balance go wrong, like the world might tilt.

At the old fenceline their breath eased. At the truck Hank sat behind the wheel with both hands locked at ten and two, staring through the windshield like he could still see the shape in the trees. Lyle closed the door gently. He did not speak when the engine turned and the heater pushed warm air over their hands. He watched the woods recede in the mirror.

He did not tell himself it was a trick or a suit. He felt the ache in his legs and the sting at his nose and the wet on his own thigh and the throb in his chest and knew whatever had looked him in the eye back there had chosen to let him leave.

He put his palm on the warped barrel across the back seat and felt the bend with his skin. Only then did he let his breath go all the way out.

CHAPTER 19

Aday later, as the pale light of morning morning crept across the ground, patchy snow clung only in the shadows while the three moved along a ridge and looked down on a clearing. Below, a pack of wolves worked an old elk with hard precision. Gray bodies fanned and closed, tongues lolling, breath steaming. One harried the flank, another darted for the hamstring, a third went at the throat when the elk stumbled. Teeth found meat. The elk's last breath rattled from its lungs and came out white in the cold.

Matto watched without moving. He waited until the legs went slack and the eyes turned to glass. Then he walked down from the ridge and stepped into the feeding pack. Heads snapped up. Lips curled. One wolf rushed and went for his thigh. Matto answered with a short backhand that sent it yelping into brush and snow. Two more feinted from opposite sides, growls rolling in their chests. Matto did not turn his shoulders. He kept walking. His size and calm drew a low, uneasy whine from the circle.

The alpha held the center a moment longer, muzzle red, hackles up. It paced once, testing him, teeth bared, and gave a hard, clipped bark. Matto closed the space by a step. The alpha backed one pace, then another, never breaking his stare, and slipped to the treeline.

The pack broke but did not flee. They lingered at the edge, weaving between trunks, eyes bright with fury and fear, tails high, ready to rush if his back ever showed. From the ridge, Kara stood still, hand on Brak's forearm to keep him there, both of them listening to the wolves' low music ride the cold.

Matto stooped. He took the elk by the jaw hinge and the base of the skull and wrenched. Vertebrae popped like wet sticks. He tore the head free, then ripped away the forelegs with slow, patient strength that made the wolves flatten their ears. He left head and legs in the snow for them and lifted the carcass to his shoulder. A few wolves slunk forward to claim what he had dropped, casting quick looks at his back. None dared close.

He climbed back to the ridge with the weight settled against him and set the carcass down where the wind would not carry the scent far. They ate fast, hands slick, teeth cracking tendon, hunger pushing them to work until only bone and gristle stayed.

By the next afternoon the forest thinned. From a high ridge they could see far into the distance, where jagged peaks rose light against the sky. The wind swept down with dry grass in it and a sharper resin than the woods behind. Matto, Kara, and Brak stood together, silent, each feeling the pull of that far land.

CHAPTER 20

Night was full when the three stopped on a ridge. The air was crisp and still, the forest below locked in shadow. A dark cleft in the rock caught Matto's attention, and he moved toward it without a sound. He ducked inside, nostrils flaring as he drew in the scents. After a moment he grunted, the sound carrying back to Kara and Brak. *"Safe."*

The cave was dry and wide enough for them to rest. From its mouth, the ridge overlooked a sweeping valley. Along the lip, a fringe of saplings, lodgepole and aspen, stood thick, with scattered stone between their trunks, before the ground yielded to the long slope. On the far side, pale shapes rose high against the starlit sky, their peaks jagged and faint with ice.

Brak stood there a long while. After four and a half hard months, a thought rose unbidden: *maybe this was where they stopped for good.* He turned his head and chattered, *"Will we stay here?"*

Matto grunted again, *"Not yet known."*

They settled in the cave, tucking themselves into the warmer shadows. While Kara and Brak rested, Matto slipped away into the trees. The forest swallowed him, his footfalls vanishing among the soft mounds of scattered snow and the quiet trunks. Hours passed.

Brak had begun to drowse when a brittle crunch outside roused him. Matto returned, shoulders heavy with a deer slung across his back. He lowered it and split the hide, passing meat to Kara and Brak in turn. They ate until the cold air lost its bite.

Beyond the cave mouth, the mountains stood silent across the valley. The hairless ones called them the Bighorn Mountains. The peaks rose like the old bones of the world, bright and cold, and even the Sasquatch went still at that beauty.

CHAPTER 21

Late morning laid a bright band across the cave mouth while the rest kept its cool dim. From the ridge path the cave was hidden under a shoulder of stone and scrub. Wind moved in steady runs across the high ground, sighing over rock and sparse pine.

Matto lay near the entrance with his back to the wall, chest rising and falling in slow breaths. His arms were loose, head tilted, a rest he allowed himself only when air and stone told him nothing hunted them. His ear flicked now and then at small sounds. He did not drop that habit, even when still.

Kara woke sore in hips and shoulders. She stood and went to work on their sleeping place. She stepped outside, not toward the rim but to the sheltered side where small pines grew in a dip. There she snapped spruce boughs from low branches, gathered long grass where the last snow thinned, and shook old needles loose. She worked fast, bundling green sprays under one arm. When the weight felt right she returned to the cave, stooped, and spread them in a loose mat. The green scent rose at once, bright and clean. Then she went out again for another load.

Brak lingered at the entrance while she worked, shifting from foot to foot. The sky pulled at him. The valley pulled harder. Matto's eyes were closed. Kara returned with a second bundle and gave Brak a quick side look, then made a soft grunt that meant go if you must, but keep your mind with your feet. Brak lifted his chin, trying to look older than he was. He gave a short click that meant he understood. Then he ducked outside and into the light.

The stone apron in front of the cave felt wide at first, a gray sheet patched with old snow and scattered grit. Brak moved along it with quick steps, nose working at the cool air. It was sharp with resin and old elk and the high, clean smell that comes when snow is going. The wind lifted the hair along his arms. He glanced back once at the cave and saw only the dark slit of its mouth under the lip of rock, safe and hidden from the drop.

He followed the curve of the ridge where the apron tapered. Pines tilted from the slope below, roots biting into cracks, their needles whispering. The valley opened like a bowl cut by a thin thread of water. The mountains beyond stood jagged and still. It was not like the wet woods they had left. There the trees stood tight, and the air was heavy. Here the sky opened, stone showed its ribs, and sight ran far. Brak stared, open eyed.

Tracks dotted a thin, wind-scoured patch of snow and he pressed his palm into a print, tasting the air. Rabbit, not fresh. He followed anyway. Matto had taught him that following mattered even when it did not feed you. The trail ran the crest, tucked into scrub near a hump of stone, then ended in a cold hollow; he dug with his fingers, found nothing, and rose with a low huff.

The ridge narrowed, and the stone fell away on both sides, steep enough that a stumble would run on and on. Ahead, a white lip of old snow crusted past the true edge, a trick for the eyes. He should have watched his feet, but the open valley pulled at him. He stepped onto the crust. It held. Another step. The wind shifted and a hairline crack whispered under his toes.

Too late. The lip sagged and his weight met nothing. The world tipped, thin sheets of old snow slid and took his feet. His arms flew wide and a raw sound climbed his throat. His left hand struck a pine trunk clinging to the rim, splinters driving under his nails, while his right caught a wrist-thick branch that bent with a long creak. One foot swung in space. The other skated across smooth rock, scraped at a seam, and held for a heartbeat.

He held his breath and pulled. Bark cut his palms. The branch groaned and began to give. Cold brushed his face as more of the thin crust sloughed away and fell in a brief veil that thinned and was gone. Small stones rattled down and only after a long count did a faint clatter come back. He pressed his chest to the trunk, cheek to bark, sap sweet in his nose. Toes felt for the smallest jut. Leaning into it, he slid his right hand higher, hooked his forearm, hugged the tree hard, and lifted until his belly came flat to rock and his knees dragged up.

He lay with his chest to the stone and his arms locked around the trunk. When he lifted his head he studied the broken lip, scalloped and dirty, harmless-looking and false, and let the lesson root deep. When the shaking eased he kept his belly low and edged away a hand at a time, old crust crackling under him, toes following the seam, and only when the ridge widened did he sit back against the trunk with his feet on honest ground. He watched the wind comb the pines and refused the lean the valley asked of him. He grunted a quiet thanks toward the tree.

He rose and traced the ridge back, staying on bare stone

and giving every white lip a wide berth. When the apron came under his feet his shoulders dropped and his gaze stayed on his steps. The cave mouth waited dark under its shelf of rock.

Inside, Kara knelt on fresh green and shook out another layer. She had made three trips to the sheltered dip, each time skirting the rim and listening for sounds. On the last, a thin cry rode the wind, hawk, fox, or Brak, so she stood and waited until only the hush of trees came back and no fear scent, then carried on. When Brak ducked through the entrance, sweat and sap and the sharp tang of old snow clung to him. Her eyes found the red on his palms. Her mouth curled into a small, crooked smile and she chattering softly, *"Careless, but breathing."*

Brak tried to look past her to the far wall as if nothing had happened. The pine mat looked soft and smelled clean. He wanted to sink into it and disappear. He lowered himself on the edge of it instead, elbows on knees, and rubbed his thumb along the sticky lines of sap on his fingers. He kept his eyes on the floor until the shake went out of them.

Matto opened his eyes. He had not moved for a long while and yet he had not been truly sleeping. He took in Brak's hands, the sap, the way his shoulders sat high and tight. He did not ask. He chattered low, *"Watch what holds you. Watch what does not."*

Brak nodded and dropped his gaze farther.

Kara carried her last armful of green to the mat, spreading it in wide sweeps. Needle tips pricked her palms through her hair. She pushed the boughs until they lay in a thick layer the length of her body and Matto's. Then she stepped outside again and returned with long grass and a handful of dry fern she had found under an overhang. She braided the grass in quick twists and wove it through the boughs to keep them from slipping. When she finished, the bed had a little spring and did not slide like loose brush. She pressed her palm into it and grunted once, satisfied.

She sat. The resin smell was strong and soothing. It clung in the air and took hold of the cold stone under it. Brak shifted closer to the mat and let his weight sink into the green. He breathed in and felt his chest loosen. The image of the broken white lip tried to push back into his mind. He let it come and sit there because it made the ground under him feel even more real.

After a time he rose and went to the cave mouth again. He did not step out. He stood in the gap and looked along the stone apron toward the place where the ridge narrowed. He could not see the tree that had held him. He knew where it was anyway. He made a small promise inside himself that he would learn that ridge the way he learned a trail to water. He would count his steps from the cave to the bend. He would mark the seams in the rock with the pads of his toes until his feet knew them without a look. The valley could pull at him again. His feet would answer it with knowledge.

Matto watched him from inside with a heavy-lidded gaze and said nothing. He let the small one measure the opening and the slope and the angle of light himself. Lessons took root deeper when you planted them with your own hands.

Kara lay back on the mat and stretched. The work had warmed her. The cave held the day's cold at the edges, but the mat was a barrier, and its scent took her mind to green places beyond snow. She turned her head and studied Brak's profile. He had returned with his pride scuffed, and that was not always a bad thing. Scuffed pride made room for care.

She lifted her hand and flicked two fingers, a gesture that meant come sit, eat, rest. Brak came and sat. She pressed a knob of dried meat into his palm, the last bit from the deer Matto had brought the night before. He took it and chewed, jaw working, eyes fixed on nothing. When he finished he licked sap and blood from his hand and made a face at the taste. Kara snorted a quiet laugh in her chest.

Time moved in small sounds. Pine needles settling. Wind drawing lines over the ridge and breaking them again. A distant raven spoke once and was silent. The sun slid lower and the light inside the cave shifted from thin white to a duller gray.

Outside, the ridge kept its long watch over the valley. Night did not rush in. It came on the way cold comes, little by little, until you notice your breath and the stone and the air have all agreed upon the same quiet.

Brak's last waking thought was not of falling. It was of the tree under his hands and his mother's hand on his shoulder long ago. One had cared. One had not. Both had held him. He made a quiet promise to both that he would keep his eyes on the ground between him and the open sky.

CHAPTER 22

Brak fidgeted at the cave mouth, shifting his feet and rolling his shoulders, then paced the stone apron again. For three days the cave had been their shelter while Matto and Kara took turns hunting, and Kara kept the bedding fresh and let him carry what she would. New land lay below and he was young and restless, his eyes always slipping to the valley, wanting to learn its lines and paths.

This morning it would not let him be. Matto's gaze had told him nothing more than its usual weight, a warning always there, and Kara had given him a sideways glance that meant be cautious, not reckless. That was enough permission.

Only in shadowed pockets along the ridge did old snow hold, thin and gray. Brak left the cave with long strides, shoulders tight with a kind of excitement he could not name.

He followed the curve of the ridge where the stone narrowed, but instead of stopping where the drop sharpened, he searched along the slope for another way and crouched, fingers brushing a thin crust in shade until he found a seam where boulders had tumbled long ago. Between them lay a steep cut filled with scrub and loose earth.

He tested it. The crust shifted, but the stone beneath held, and Brak set his jaw and began to descend. His toes dug for purchase and his hands grabbed branches where they grew; he slid more than once, bark scraping his palms, but each time he caught himself. His breath puffed white around his face, and when he reached the bottom his chest swelled with a mix of triumph and nerves.

The trees thickened here, tall spruce standing close together, their shadows long even in daylight. Brak's ears twitched at every creak of branch as he moved slower, inhaling the scents layered in the air. Deer, squirrel, the faint musk of wolf though not fresh. He pressed his nose to the ground where paw marks crossed a shaded strip.

A creek cut through the valley floor. Where the spruce closed in, thin sheets of ice still held; elsewhere the water ran dark and quick. Brak stepped onto the bank and crouched to look at tracks pressed into a skim of ice along the shaded edge. Elk, maybe two days old; a fox, more recent. He traced each with a fingertip, head bent in concentration.

He stood then, eyes on the ground as he walked along the water, following the shallow bends while his thoughts wandered. He imagined telling Kara what he found, showing Matto the exact place where elk crossed, and perhaps hearing the grunt that meant approval.

Brak lifted his head at the same moment the air shifted, and his body froze.

Ahead, where the creek narrowed into a trail lined with spruce, a hairless one stood.

She was female. He knew by the shape, by the smaller frame compared to the hairless ones he had glimpsed before. She wore heavy cloth wrapped close to her body, a hood pushed back so her light hair showed, and her wide eyes locked on him without a blink, transfixed. She did not move, and the cold breeze carried the sharp tang of her scent to him, fear and surprise and something else too.

Brak tilted his head, studying her. His body did not lurch forward or back; curiosity pinned him where he stood. She was unlike the hairless ones. A small axe hung from one of her hands, the head dull with cold, as though she had been cutting at branches before he appeared.

For a long breath neither moved, the forest around them hushed in anticipation.

Brak blinked, his head lowering slightly. He could feel his heart but it did not pound like when the ridge had nearly claimed him. This was different. He wanted to understand her face, the way her mouth hung open, the way her shoulders trembled, and he gave a soft click in his throat, not meant for her, meant for himself, a sound of thought.

The female's chest rose sharp and fast. She stared without blinking, held as if fixed to a point.

Then, sudden and small, her hands faltered; the axe slipped from her fingers and struck a shaded drift with a muffled thud, the blade sinking into white.

The sound snapped something in her. She turned and bolted down the trail, feet punching through the drift, arms flailing once as she vanished into thicker trees, branches shaking in her wake before they stilled.

Brak remained where he was, eyes on the place where she had been and ears straining for the fading sound of her steps. He lifted his chin and pulled in her scent as it drifted away, and then it was gone.

He stood in silence for a long while, breath pluming softly

and curling around him. The axe lay half-buried in the shaded drift where she had dropped it, and when Brak walked to it and crouched, the handle felt smooth and smelled faintly of her hands; he sniffed it, then left it where it had fallen.

Turning away, he retraced his path along the creek back toward the slope. His feet carried him faster than before, not from fear but from a strange buzzing inside him.

The climb up was harder than the descent. Thin crust in shadow gave and rocks slipped beneath his toes, but he hauled himself upward, breath ragged, until the stone apron came under his feet and his shoulders ached. He paused, looking back over the valley once before slipping into the cave.

Kara glanced up from where she sat, her eyes flicking over him. She studied his face but asked nothing. Matto's eyes opened, their dark weight holding him in place. Brak ducked his head, grunted low, and sat in silence.

****

That night the valley spread dark below the ridge. Brak sat on a ledge above the drop, shoulders pressed to stone, and squinted at two faint pinpricks on the valley floor. Two dwellings of the hairless ones, one nearer and another farther down the valley. The lights shimmered and flickered, and curiosity stirred; hairless ones had always fascinated him, yet he knew from the few years behind him that going near them could be dangerous He wondered if the female at the creek was a good hairless one or not.

He stayed there a long time, watching. He did not move. His thoughts drifted.

He remembered his mother. The way she had watched him climb trees. The way she had pulled him close when he had fallen from a tree after losing his grip. He wondered what she would say now, after all this time. He felt her absence like a hollow under his ribs.

Brak's eyes stayed on the lights in the valley until Kara came back with an elk to share.

CHAPTER 23

The back door banged against the frame as Alice burst inside, boots leaving streaks of mud across the wooden floor. She was breathing roughly, her face flushed with crimson.

At the table, her husband, John, looked up from his folded newspaper. A pencil sat in his hand, paused above a crossword grid. His eyes narrowed.

"What's the matter with you, Hun?" he asked, his voice edge with concern.

She tore at the zipper of her jacket, fingers fumbling. The heavy coat slid from her shoulders in a heap on the bench. She pressed both hands to the table to steady herself, and lowered her head as she tried to drag air into her lungs.

"I was out back," she said finally, voice unsteady.

"Walking the trail down by the creek."

He set the pencil down, the eraser tapping the wood once. "And?"

She lifted her head, eyes wide. "I looked up and saw a sasquatch."

His brow pulled together. "In the daytime?"

"Yes," she snapped, sharper than she meant. She swallowed and sat down heavily across from him, arms folding tight across her chest. "Clear as I'm looking at you right now."

He leaned back slowly in his chair, eyes never leaving hers.

"What did it look like?" he asked.

She rubbed her forehead with her hand, trying to calm herself. "It wasn't full grown. A young one, maybe a juvenile. About five and a half feet tall. Not much taller than me, really." Her eyes drifted, as if she were seeing it again. "The look on its face… it was curious, I think. Almost a little scared. You know how a dog tilts its head? It did that. I don't think it knew what to do with me."

He sat forward. "What did it do? Was it aggressive?"

She shook her head quickly. "No. It just stood there staring at me. But it still freaked me out, being that close. I could see every bit of its face, its arms, the way it breathed. I was so shocked I dropped my axe and ran as fast as my legs would let me."

His mouth pressed into a line, thoughtful. "You think it's one of the ones that have been coming around our property at night?"

She hesitated. Her fingers tightened around her sleeve. "I don't know."

The words lingered heavy in the room. She looked towards the window as a chill ran up her spine.

CHAPTER 24

The ridge carried a sharp wind the next morning, scraping Brak's face and tugging at the hair along his arms. He kept below the skyline on a narrow ledge under the crest, letting rock break his shape as he moved its length; the stone lay wide at first, then narrowed to a shoulder that looked across the valley floor.

His eyes roved below, scanning for deer, elk, any shift of life. Something moved. Brak stilled and sank lower into the stone's shadow as a figure stepped from a square-walled dwelling. It was the same female hairless one he had seen days before at the creek, moving with a hurried step and drawing her heavy cloth close as she crossed the open ground.

Another hairless one, broader in the shoulders, stood nearby. Brak watched them both with curiosity gnawing at his chest. The female walked to a metal beast with four round feet. It growled low as she climbed inside, the door slamming shut, and then it rolled along a long strip of cleared earth. Brak followed it with his eyes until it slipped between trees, the sound fading.

****

That evening Matto returned with a deer slung over his shoulder. He dropped it just inside the cave, the heavy thud echoing off stone. They ate quickly, tearing at the warm meat, but Brak's thoughts were not on the meal. His eyes drifted to the ridge again and again.

When the last of the bones lay scattered, Brak slipped out into the night air. The valley stretched below, quiet and black, only the faint glow of lights from the hairless one's dwellings showing against the dark. Restlessness churned inside him. He sat on the ridge edge, knees pulled close, his eyes searching the world beneath.

Kara joined him, settling on her haunches beside him. She watched him for a moment in silence before speaking.

She chattered, *"You do not sit still."*

"It's never been my way," Brak replied.

He kept his eyes on the valley and chattered, *"Tell me about your mother."*

Kara's gaze shifted, distant. She replied, *"I do not remember her."*

The words were plain, carrying no weight of anger or grief. Just fact. Still, they left Brak with an ache. He lowered his eyes, thinking of his own mother, of the emptiness that now lived in its place.

Before he could speak again, movement caught his eyes.

He tensed, leaning forward. From the black line of trees at the far edge of the valley, four figures broke free. They ran fast, their shapes hunched and powerful. Brak's heart quickened. These were not deer or wolves. They moved with the same weight he carried in his own body.

The figures darted across open ground and hid behind the metal beasts and the wooden barn near the dwelling. For a moment all was still. Then the first stone flew.

It struck the side of the dwelling with a hard crack.

Another followed, then another, until the air below churned with the thud and crash of rock on wood and glass. The hairless ones' home shuddered under the blows, and the sound climbed the valley in broken echoes that reached the ridge.

Brak shot to his feet. He grunted, *"We should help."*

Kara grabbed his arm, her grip strong. She chattered, *"No. Matto would want us to stay out of it."*

Brak snarled low, eyes flashing. He grunted, *"But they attack."*

Kara held his gaze, steady and firm. She replied, *"It is not our fight."*

Below, sudden bursts of brightness flared from the dwelling, harsh white beams spilling into the dark. The glow spread across the ground and walls, making the attackers scatter and shift with the restless movement of beings caught between the wild and the thinking world.

Brak squinted. To him the beams looked like moonlight dragged from the sky and forced onto the earth, false and sharp, nothing like the calm silver above.

His chest heaved, body taut with the need to move. To do

something. But Kara did not let go, and the weight of her hand was enough to keep him rooted to the ridge.

They watched in silence as the attack carried on, the valley alive with false moonlight and violence that unsettled Brak.

He wanted to tell Kara about the female hairless one he had seen up close, the way her eyes had locked on his. But fear held him still, fear he would be in trouble for wandering too far. And deep inside he kept the thought that this hairless one had seemed good, harmless even, not like the others.

CHAPTER 25

Alice lay in bed, deep asleep, dreaming that Denzel Washington was in her kitchen flipping pancakes and handing her a spatula with a wink.

The first thud knocked the spatula from her hand. A second hit a heartbeat later and the wall gave a short, unhappy shake. The third set the window glass ticking.

Alice snapped awake, sitting up in the dark. She held her breath and listened as another bang rolled across the house, dull and solid, followed by the gritty slide of something bouncing down the siding. Somewhere a frame tapped the wall. She tried to whisper John's name, but no sound came. Another thud answered anyway.

Beside her, John groaned and swung his legs out of bed. "What the hell was that?"

The answer came at once: a loud crack, glass tinkling from the front of the house, then another heavy thud against the siding.

Alice stumbled to the window and pushed the curtain aside. The yard was black and still, the barn only a darker shape against the night. Then something slammed against the wall beneath her and she jerked back with a cry.

"Rocks," she gasped. "They're throwing rocks!"

John was already pulling on his boots. "Stay back," he said, though his voice carried more alarm than command.

The next stone struck the porch post with such force the whole frame shivered. A second later, one of the outdoor lights flicked on, bathing the yard in white. The sudden brightness swept across the ground and the barn wall. Shadows leapt, moving quick, figures ducking behind the cars and barn.

Alice pressed a hand to her mouth. "They're out there." Her voice trembled.

John grabbed the old rifle from its stand near the door, the metal clattering faintly in his hands. His face had drained of color.

The stones kept coming. Thuds rolled through the walls, each one closer to shattering something vital. Glass cracked in the kitchen window with a brittle pop. Alice could feel the house shaking under the barrage, every hit echoing through the floor.

"Why did they come back?" she whispered urgently. "It's been quiet for months and now they're terrorizing us again?"

John pulled back the curtain in the living room just enough to peer through. The bright beam from the porch light caught the movement of a heavy arm withdrawing behind the barn, then another rock arcing through the air. It smashed against the side of the house, splinters flying.

"Stay away from the glass," John said quickly, letting the curtain fall. "Looking out was a damn fool thing to do."

Alice stepped closer to him despite herself, every instinct telling her to stay back. The light hummed over the yard, showing only flickers of movement and the gleam of stones sailing out of the dark.

Each impact carried the force of something deliberate, something angry.

And Alice could not shake the image of the young one she had seen by the creek. Its eyes had been curious, not hateful.

She wondered if that same young one could be among those hurling rocks at her home.

As quickly as the rock throwing had started, it finished, and silence remained. Alice and John did not sleep a wink the rest of the night.

CHAPTER 26

Before first light, Kara found Brak asleep inside the cave, propped against the wall with a bone still in his hand. She touched his shoulder and woke him from deep sleep, then drew him into the dark trees.

She kept him moving the folds behind the cave through spruce and fir, with white-bark aspen in the damp draws where thin bark shone like old bone. In shaded pockets a skin of old snow held, but most ground showed wet needles and black soil. She taught wind first: an open palm to her face and a slow turn meant read it; two fingers cutting across her chest meant crosswind; a closed hand pressed down meant stay low. When he lifted for a better view, her hand found the back of his neck and brought him down. *"Low,"* she grunted.

They hunted in quiet arcs, keeping to timber and broken ground. Kara set the line and Brak stepped in her print, stone when she chose stone, soft duff when she wanted sound to die. She paused to let him feel the faint tremble in a spruce when elk shifted beds up-slope, then pressed his palm to a cedar-sweet rub where a bull had worked last season. At a weave of willow shoots she traced hare runs with a blunt nail and tapped two fingers to her lips. *"Later,"* she grunted. *"Meat first,"*.

Water came next. She showed him the long creek he knew and the quiet streams he did not: a cold thread seeping under a boulder into a stone bowl, a narrow tongue that vanished into moss and reappeared downslope. She made him drink and wait to hear how flow could hide a body if he moved with it and betray him if he crossed it wrong. In a collapsed bend she pushed a foot into dark silt, brought up a fat root, scraped it clean, chewed, then handed him a length. *"Good,"* she grunted.

On the second morning fresh elk sign crossed the cool side of a rise. Kara sank and became a stump, and Brak matched the shape. A cow and last year's calf ghosted the willows at forty paces. His shoulders lifted to slip forward, but her fingers touched his ribs, and he felt the meaning. Not here. They circled instead and took a young deer later in a pocket where fir closed the sky and ground fell away in three directions. They ate with neat bites and left the rest in a crease of rock for other forest animals. Kara cracked a leg against stone and pressed the white length to him, showing where to split and how to pull the thick center. *"Make you strong,"* she grunted. He finished it without complaint.

They ranged higher that afternoon under thinner trees where wind ran clean. Far across chalk shelves a small band of mountain goats stood like chips of the peaks; Kara pointed and then closed her fingers, grunting *"Look, do not chase."* In a low saddle wolves had passed in the night; she set his fingers in a track so he felt full pads and deep claws, then held his palm to the earth until the last cool of the print told its age.

At dusk she led him to a high shelf away from open ground and showed a better sleep than stone alone: spruce boughs under a fallen trunk, a pillow of moss stripped from the north sides of old stumps, a small line of rocks to blunt the first reach of wind. They lay hands flat, eyes closed and listened. Water ran steady below, an owl called once, no grit slid on stone. Safe.

As night fell they reached the cave, Matto inside with head tipped as if still listening to the day, and Kara set what they had brought near him. *"Meat,"* she grunted. Brak laid the last of it down and sat, legs heavy, mind not yet still but closer, his wanting quiet, while Kara watched him in a long silence and hoped the past days' hunts and small lessons would keep his eyes from the valley and the hairless ones below.

CHAPTER 27

The ridge lay still under the night. Stars spread endless across the black. Brak lay on his back on a narrow ledge below the crest, shoulders in stone, eyes on the sky. He traced the lights with his gaze, though he had no names for them, remembering his mother's hands lifting him toward such a sky, pointing without words as if the lights held truths she could not speak; and he heard his sister's small laugh again, water over stones, from nights under these same far sparks. The memory pulled tight under his ribs until it hurt, and he closed his eyes, breathing the faint scent of old snow and spruce until the ache settled.

A sound drifted up from the valley floor, a heavy crack against wood. Then another. Brak rolled to an elbow, ears twitching, then pushed up to sit and turned toward the distant hairless ones' dwelling. The sound grew sharper, more frequent: stones striking with furious rhythm. Wind tugged at his hair. More noises followed, heavier now: running feet, the slap of bodies against siding, thuds on the roof. They echoed across the valley, and with his keen ears Brak caught every one. His nostrils flared. The air carried their scent to him, thick and harsh, sweat and rage and the musk of bodies straining with effort. The dwelling below shuddered under the blows, though from this distance he saw only the flashes of light kindling inside. Windows glared bright against the dark like false moons, but no shapes appeared behind them.

Brak's teeth ground together. He could almost feel the fear inside those walls, the hairless ones cowering where they could not be seen.

The attack did not stop. Stones flew in a constant barrage, each impact echoing in the valley. The figures moved like shadows around the dwelling, their voices carrying in harsh grunts Brak understood too well.

His body trembled. He could not stay still. The heat in his chest forced him forward until he was already rising, already descending from the ridge. His feet found the steep path he had followed before, the stones and roots catching under his hands as he lowered himself down the face. Breath steamed in the night air as he pushed harder, sliding once, catching himself on a branch. The sounds below pulled him faster.

By the time he reached the tree line at the valley floor, his legs burned and his chest heaved. He crouched low, the dwelling ahead of him alive with strikes and thuds. Figures lunged along its edges, their silhouettes tall and wide.

Brak whistled.

The sharp note cut across the night. One of the figures froze, head snapping toward him. The others paused, then all four turned as one.

They saw him.

With a chorus of low roars they charged. Dirt exploded under their feet, their shapes massive and fast, closing the space in heartbeats. Brak stood rooted, his fists clenched, though fear curled in his belly like fire.

The first one skidded to a halt a few paces from him, breath steaming. Its head was more conical than his, brow ridges jutting heavy above yellow amber eyes, teeth bared. The others spread around, encircling him.

He grunted, *"You not belong."*

Brak swallowed but did not back away. He chattered, *"Leave hairless ones. They not hurt you."*

The second, broader than the first, stepped close, eyes hard. He replied, *"Speak like smalling. Know nothing. Go. Find own fight."*

The others stamped at the ground, growls low in their throats.

Brak's hands shook, but he forced the words out. He chattered, *"I not sit. I not watch. You hurt ones who no fight."*

The first one replied, *"Not welcome. Stay and you bleed."*

They pressed closer, the ring tightening. Brak's heart pounded, his breath fast. He braced himself though he knew he could not take all four.

A sharp huff broke through the night.

All four heads turned toward the trees. Kara stepped from the shadow line, piercing amber eyes narrow, chest rising in steady rhythm. The air hardened around her, old and heavy, and the juveniles shrank without meaning to.

She grunted, *"Brak. Come."*

The broad one leaned in, nostrils flaring. He chattered, *"Lucky, little one. She save you. Not always."*

Another jerked his chin toward the woods. He added,

"Walk. Do not return."

Brak trembled with anger and shame, but Kara's gaze held him fast. She grunted again, *"Move."*

His shoulders sagged. He took one last look at the dwelling where the false moons still burned and the walls wore fresh scars, then turned to Kara.

They slipped into the trees, the others' low growls and rough chatter fading behind them.

The climb back up the ridge dragged heavy. Brak's legs ached, his chest burned, but worse was the heat of shame inside him.

At the cave mouth Kara turned on him, eyes fierce. She chattered angrily, *"Fool. They kill you. Four on one. You almost dead."*

Brak dropped his gaze, breath unsteady. He chattered, *"I not sit. They hurt ones who not fight."*

Kara's face stayed hard, though something softer moved behind her eyes. She stepped closer, voice low. She chattered, *"I not tell Matto. Only this time. Again, I not help."*

Brak lifted his eyes. He replied, *"All on me."*

For a long moment they stood in silence, wind whispering through the trees above. Kara huffed and turned away at last, shoulders heavy.

Inside, the cave lay dark and quiet, but Brak still heard the echoes from below. Stone on wood. Harsh grunts.

He lay down and curled against the wall, eyes open. He saw again the faces of the four who had circled him. He knew the fight had only begun.

****

"Just stay down," John whispered. "Stay away from the windows."

"They're on the roof, Hun," Alice cried, clutching his arm.

The sound above them was deafening, heavy steps pounding back and forth across the shingles, shaking the beams of the dwelling. Stones cracked against the siding, some rattling down the chimney, others shattering glass. One struck the frame of the living room window, sending shards across the floor. Alice pulled her blanket tighter and crouched lower, her breath ragged.

John gripped the rifle across his knees but did not rise from where he sat against the wall. His jaw was clenched tight, his eyes fixed on the floorboards as if looking up would make things worse.

The assault came from all sides. The walls quivered with every blow. Rocks clattered on the porch, rattled across the roof, split against the barn outside. The noise was so constant Alice could not tell if there were four of them or ten. Her body shook with every strike.

"They'll break through," she whispered. "They'll smash the doors, John."

"No," he said quickly, though his voice carried little strength. "They want to scare us. That's what they do."

The words did nothing to calm her. She could hear them grunting, snarling, their weight shifting close, so close it felt as though they were right next to her.

One heavy step landed directly above them. Dust sifted from the ceiling, falling across Alice's hair. She let out a sob and buried her face against John's shoulder.

"We should have left," she said. "We should have gone when it was quiet. I cannot do this again."

John tightened his arm around her, though his hands shook. He pressed his forehead against hers and whispered, "They will get bored again, don't worry."

The pounding rose to a frenzy. Rocks crashed harder, footsteps thundered over the roof, the very frame of the dwelling groaning with the strain. Alice thought of the months of silence, the way she had begun to feel safe again, how she had almost believed the terror was behind them. That hope was gone now, stripped away in the racket.

Once again, just as suddenly as it had begun, the barrage slowed. The steps grew distant, moving off the roof. The last stone rattled across the porch and fell silent.

Alice kept her head pressed down, waiting for the next strike, but none came.

John lifted his eyes toward the broken window, breath tight in his chest. The night outside was black and still, the only sound the hiss of the wind against the walls.

"They're gone," he whispered, though even he did not sound certain. "They're gone babe."

Alice swallowed hard, her hands trembling. "Why do they do this?"

He could not answer. He only held her tighter, staring at the window, hoping they would not come back.

CHAPTER 28

Early the next morning, the road ran long and empty under a washed-out sky. Alice kept both hands tight on the wheel, eyes on the blacktop while her mind drifted far. The groceries in the back seat slid and bumped on the curves, but she barely noticed.

She had driven this road for years. Once it had been peaceful, the same wide fields and the same dark treelines unrolling past. Now every mile felt heavier, a slow climb into dread. She could not look at the trees without imagining shapes threaded between them. Tall, hairy bodies. Watching eyes.

Her stomach tightened as she thought back to the beginning. Four months ago, the nights first filled with strange calls, long howls not like wolves, then raw screams that rose and tore at the dark. After that came pebbles ticking the siding, soft thuds on the roof, something moving where no light could catch it. They decided it was kids, trespassers, maybe animals they had not dealt with before. It did not stop. It grew worse with every night.

It took weeks to say out loud what they were. Weeks of heavy steps outside the windows, of screams rolling across the valley, of waking to dead raccoons set on the porch and broad footprints pressed in the snow. Neither of them wanted to say the word. Then they saw the figures themselves and there was no denying it. Sasquatch.

They had lived on this land ten years without trouble, only the odd bear nosing around now and then. Why now, why them, they had no idea.

They fought it the ways they knew. Floodlights snapped the yard to daylight, cameras went up on poles and trees. It did not matter. The cameras shifted or crashed to earth; sometimes rocks spidered the lenses until they went blind. The lights changed nothing. On nights when the yard stayed quiet, Alice still woke from dreams of pounding on the roof and hands at the glass, heart racing like she had been running.

Both Alice and John saw them close. Not just shadows, not just a roar in the dark. Faces. Shapes. Broad shoulders caught in the porch-lamp glow. They came right up to the windows, breath fogging the glass, and they were the ugliest things either of them had ever seen: heavy brows, flat noses, wide mouths pressed to the pane as if to taste the room. Other times they darted through the yard, huge bodies slipping out of sight the instant you tried to focus.

John nearly fired more than once, rifle in hand and finger tight on the trigger, but Alice begged him not to. She feared a shot would only bring more of them crashing down on the house.

They terrified her; she would say so. John would not. He held himself stiff and insisted he was fine, that she was frightened enough for both of them. She knew better. She saw how his eyes moved when the howls rose from the trees. She heard the quick catch in his breath when the knocks echoed out, hard and hollow, like a club on a trunk.

Their nearest neighbor was nearly a mile away and there only half the year. They had no one to lean on. Alice searched online and found a local group that claimed to study Sasquatch. She called. They came and sat in their trucks at the edge of the property, walked the yard once or twice, took a few pictures, and climbed back in. When rocks began to pepper their truck that night, they drove off fast and never returned. Later, Alice mentioned it to a local friend, and the woman laughed, sure it was a joke. After that she told no one else, and neither did John.

The harassment ran seven long weeks. Every other night, without fail. At first, they replaced the cracked panes, and the ones blown clean through; by the third week the cost bit hard, so they screwed boards over the frames and called it temporary. By then no one stepped outside after dark.

Then, as suddenly as it had begun, it stopped.

Silence. Weeks of it. Enough that Alice started to believe it was over. She even began to feel safe again.

But now they were back.

The thought made her chest tight as the trees closed in around the road. The driveway wound narrow between the pines, climbing toward the house. The air seemed to thicken here. Even in daylight the trees crowded close, leaning like they held secrets.

She thought of the young one she had seen by the frozen creek. Small, not much taller than herself, its eyes curious more than cruel. She had told John it looked afraid, and she had meant it. But what if she had been wrong? What if that face was the same one in the dark, hurling stones at her walls? She could not decide if it had been innocent or only waiting to grow into the same terror as the others.

She pulled into the drive and slowed, her breath catching in her throat. Something was there, propped against the wooden step.

She shut the engine off, the sudden quiet heavy in her ears. Her hands trembled as she opened the door. Cold air rushed in, sharper now, biting her cheeks. She stepped onto the gravel, as she checked her surroundings before her eyes focussed on the porch.

Her axe. The one she had dropped that day by the creek.

Her heart hammered. She froze at the edge of the drive, staring. The handle leaned neatly against the railing, the blade glinting in the morning light. She felt the blood drain from her face.

Slowly she raised her eyes to the tree line. The trees stood silent, their branches still. She could not see anything between them, no movement, no flash of shape.

Her breath came shallow. Did one of them bring it back? Did that young one carry it here, careful not to be seen?

She stepped onto the porch, her boots hollow on the boards. She reached out and touched the handle, her fingers brushing the wood. It was cold, damp from the air. She lifted it slowly, her eyes never leaving the trees.

Was this a warning? A sign she had been too close? Or was it something else?

Her thoughts circled. Could there be good and bad among them? The ones that tore at her roof in the night, and another that bent down to return what she had lost. She did not know what to believe. She only knew the fear that had grown inside her, twisting tighter with each passing day.

She turned, clutching the axe, and opened the door. Inside the house was quiet. John would not be home for hours. She shut the door behind her and leaned her back against it, the axe still in her hand. The groceries could wait.

CHAPTER 29

The forest called in small voices: birdsong, wing brush, a distant bark swallowed by trees. Kara worked at the bedding in the cave, pulling old needles and adding new, making the hollow tight and clean. Matto slept heavy in the back, breath slow, body spent from the hunt before sunup. Brak stood at the mouth, watching a squirrel flick through the brush below.

Curiosity tugged. He drifted down the ridge, keeping to brush and rock, moving the way Matto had shown him but not as well. He followed the treeline where shadow lay, slipping from cedar to stone and on again. He wandered, curious. The low ground opened here and there into breaks that held the scent of hairless ones and the thin, stale trace of their strange metal beasts. He kept to cover. He listened.

A twig snapped behind him.

He turned too slow. Weight hit him from the side and took him off his feet. The world rolled. He saw hair, long and dark, a young face bared with its teeth. A forearm drove under his chin. Claws raked his ribs. He shoved up with both hands, but another body hit his back and drove him to the ground.

They were four. The same four. He felt it in the way they moved together, fast and sure, practice written into every shift of weight.

Brak twisted, got a knee under him, and drove his head into a chest. The body grunted and slid. He rolled and came up on a crouch. A hand caught his wrist and bent it back until his palm opened. A blow clipped the side of his face and sent light across his eyes. He planted and swung anyway, catching a shoulder with a short hook that made his arm throb.

"Small one does not learn," one chattered, breath hot.

Another gave a short, mean laugh. *"Not your fight. Not your place."*

Brak did not answer. He set his feet the way Matto had taught him and waited for the next rush.

It came low. He met it with a forearm, but the second body struck a blink after, high and hard, and they took him back together. A hand closed in his hair and yanked. He clawed at the grip and tore free some of his own hair to turn and drive an elbow into a rib. A hiss. Then fingers closed around his thigh and lifted.

He rose clean off the ground. The trunk met his back like stone and took his breath. White crowded the edges of his sight. He slid down the bark, hands searching for purchase, legs refusing to hold him.

He pushed to stand. One stepped in and hammered his chest. He dropped again. A heel thudded into his side. Fire ran around his ribs. He tasted iron. Hands caught his shoulders and shook him once, almost playful.

"Go back to your cave," one grunted.

"Find your own fight," another chattered. *"Stay away. Or we do more than make you bleed."*

They let him fall against the tree and moved off, four shapes turning to the brush and vanishing with a quiet learned over many nights. He listened until even the small sounds faded.

He sat with his spine to the trunk, arm bleeding where claws had raked, hair sticking in damp lines to his face. The ache inside his chest spread and settled. He lowered his head and thought of his mother, the way her arms had wrapped his sister even in death, hands cut and bloody, fighting to the last. He thought of how he had failed her and closed his eyes, letting the pain wash until it dulled.

Up on the ridge, Kara finished the bedding and stepped to the edge of the overhang, wondering where Brak had gone. The wind shifted. She caught his scent and, under it, the sharp stink of the four. She did not call. She moved.

She went fast along the slope, weight soft on stone, angle sure. The forest quieted around her, a jay scolding once and then falling still. She dropped into the lower brush and found the churn in the duff where bodies had hit. Blood threaded the air, thin and fresh.

Brak was slumped against a tree, eyes open, mouth tight. He tried to push himself up when he saw her. His arms shook. They did not lift him.

Kara did not speak. She slid an arm under his and set her hip to take his weight. He stood with her help and leaned without meaning to. They took two slow steps; she stopped and put her hand flat on his chest to hold him steady while his balance returned, then they climbed.

It took time. The slope made his breath ragged and the

pain in his ribs sharp. Kara took more of his weight at the steeper cut, dragging him the last short rise to the overhang. She eased him down onto the bedding she had just made. He closed his eyes, opened them again as if to speak, then did not.

She cleaned the claw marks with damp moss and pressed the edges together with her thumbs. She wrapped his forearm with long strips of hide, binding snug but not tight. Her fingers checked his ribs, reading pain in his breath and the small flinch he tried to hide.

He watched her hands. He said nothing.

Brak slept through the half-light and into dusk. When he woke, the pain had settled into a wide ache. He did not try to stand. He lay on his side and looked at the mouth of the cave and the slice of sky beyond it.

Twilight gathered. Matto stirred in the back and rose. He stood over Brak a long breath, reading the new marks, jaw working once. He turned to go.

Kara's eyes followed him to the mouth. She waited until he stood with his hand on stone, then chattered, *"He went down. Alone. He finds trouble because he wants right."*

Matto did not turn. He chattered, *"Not our fight. We owe hairless ones nothing."*

Kara's voice stayed low and even. She chattered, *"I know. But he does not turn from right. He sees it and moves. He will do it again."*

Matto's hand flexed against the rock. He replied, *"He will walk into danger. He will not come back."*

Kara drew a breath. She grunted, *"Will you help."*

He stood very still. Far below, small lights held like cold embers that never died. He chattered, *"We walk many moons to find a place. I do not ruin it. We keep to ourselves. He will learn the hard way."*

Kara's gaze went to Brak. The young one watched them both without lifting his head.

Matto stepped into the dark to hunt.

Kara settled by Brak and sat close. He lay quiet, the hurt in him spreading and thinning and finally going heavy. Brush whispered outside the mouth.

Brak did not sleep right away. He watched the slice of sky and thought of the four and of his mother. A small sound rose in his throat and he held it there so it would not turn into something else. When sleep came, it came fast and without dreams.

Morning showed only a smear of thin cloud and frost on the ground. Brak woke stiff and sore, the bindings tacky where blood had dried. Kara checked the wraps and nodded once. No words. He sat up slow and tested his ribs with a breath. They held.

He looked at the mouth of the cave and swallowed hard. He looked at Kara and grunted, *"I am sorry."*

She shook her head once. She grunted, *"Heal. Learn."*

He lowered his eyes. He would.

CHAPTER 30

Rock at his spine and the cave dark behind him, Brak sat on the ground with his knees up, arms loose over them. The fight days before still lived in his bones. Bruises were deep. Cuts pulled when he moved. He breathed steady, each breath catching a little.

He set one palm to earth and traced slow lines with a single finger, his thoughts moving in the same circles. He had not told Matto or Kara what truly pulled him down there. He had not told them about the hairless one by the creek. The secret sat like a stone in him. He wanted to speak it, and he was afraid.

Behind him, in the dark of the cave, Matto stirred. The big one's weight shifted, a rumble rising in his chest as he pushed himself upright. He blinked at the bright light outside, his broad shoulders framed in shadow. He grunted, not a word but enough for Brak to turn his head.

Matto grunted, *"Come."*

Brak rose at once. His legs still felt heavy, but eagerness cut through the pain. He wanted Matto's approval more than he wanted rest. He followed as Matto climbed the rock beside the cave and took that way. At the far edge Matto dropped without a sound, landing light and already moving. Brak scrambled up and jumped after him; his feet hit hard and he slapped a hand to the stone to steady before he caught up.

They walked in silence for a long while, their steps steady across the frost-hardened ground. The forest thinned as they took the slope, then opened into a wide clearing where the earth was bare and hard.

Matto stopped at the center. He grunted, *"Find rocks."*

Brak tilted his head. He grunted, *"Rocks?"*

Matto's eyes narrowed. He replied, *"Rocks. Many. Bring."*

Brak's chest quickened. He hurried off, crouching low, scanning the ground. He gathered what he could find, fistfuls of stones, some small and smooth, others jagged. He carried them back and dropped them at Matto's feet, then rushed to fetch more. His sore muscles pulled at him, but he ignored the ache. Soon a small pile grew between them, gray and brown, cold to the touch.

Matto crouched, picking up one stone. He weighed it in his palm, then glanced at Brak. He grunted, *"Throw."*

Brak blinked. He grunted, *"Throw?"*

Matto stood, his arm moving in a sudden arc. The stone left his hand fast, cutting through the air. It struck the trunk of a pine at the far side of the clearing with a heavy crack, bark splintering from the blow. The sound echoed into the trees. Matto grunted low, satisfied. He pointed to the pile. He grunted, *"You. Throw."*

Brak's eyes widened. His chest swelled with excitement. He snatched a stone from the pile and turned toward the tree. He threw with all his might. The rock spun awkward, flying high, and struck the ground far short of the trunk.

Matto's brow lowered. He grunted, *"No."* He stepped closer, his arm motion sharp as he mimed the movement. He grunted, *"Straight. Strong. Fast. Not weak."*

Brak nodded quickly, eager. He grabbed another stone and hurled it. This one flew harder but veered wide, missing the tree completely.

Matto's jaw tightened. He grunted, *"Again."*

Brak tried again. And again. The stones flew, but most fell short or missed wide. His arm ached from the effort, his breath fast with frustration. He turned to Matto, his face tight, but the older one only stared at him, stern and steady.

Matto grunted, *"Again."*

Brak bit his lip and fetched more stones. He threw until his shoulder burned, until sweat dampened the hair at his temples despite the cold. His stones cracked against the earth, snapping twigs, bouncing away. Rarely did one come near the trunk.

Matto watched with stillness, though the flicker of impatience glimmered in his eyes. At last he stepped forward, grabbed a stone, and crouched. He held the rock out before Brak. He grunted, *"Watch."*

He shifted his stance, his weight on one leg, the other braced. His arm moved in a smooth line, his wrist snapping at the end. The stone flew fast, striking the trunk again with a sharp crack. He turned his head toward Brak. He grunted, *"See."*

Brak swallowed and nodded. He took a stone, copying the stance. His legs spread wide, his arm pulled back. He hurled it. The stone flew truer this time, striking just beside the tree, bouncing into the brush.

Matto's lips pressed into a thin line. He did not praise, but he did not scold. He only grunted, *"Better."*

Brak's chest lifted. A flicker of pride stirred in him. He grabbed another stone, tried again. This one hit closer, thudding against the bark low near the roots.

He turned quickly, searching Matto's face for approval.

The big one only nodded once, curt. He grunted, *"More."*

Brak set his jaw and fetched more stones. He threw again and again, his arms aching, his back tight. Some missed, but more began to strike close to the tree. Each crack of stone on bark sent a thrill through his chest. He was learning. Slowly, painfully, but learning.

When the pile of smaller stones was gone, Matto turned away without a word. He strode to the edge of the clearing and bent low, his massive hands gripping larger, heavier rocks. He carried them back and dropped them at Brak's feet with a dull thud. He grunted, *"These. Throw."*

Brak's eyes widened. He bent, straining to lift one. The weight dragged at his arm, pulled at his shoulder, but he clenched his teeth and hurled it with all his might. The stone arced slow, heavy, striking the tree low with a deep thud.

Matto's eyes narrowed, watching closely. He grunted, *"Again."*

Brak bent for another, his hands slipping on its rough surface. He pulled it up, chest straining, breath rasping through his teeth. He swung his arm, legs unsteady, and the stone left his hand. It struck short, bouncing hard against the roots of the pine.

He staggered forward, almost falling. His arms quivered. He looked to Matto, shame tugging at him.

Matto only grunted, *"Again."*

Brak swallowed, his throat dry. He bent once more, every muscle screaming as he lifted another rock. It felt like lifting a piece of the ridge itself. His knees shook, his back pulled tight, but he held it high and heaved it forward. This time the stone crashed against the trunk with a hollow crack.

Brak dropped to one knee, panting, his chest burning, arms trembling with the weight of it. He wanted to stop. Every part of him ached, every breath felt sharp. Yet when he looked up, Matto's eyes were fixed on him, steady and unyielding.

Brak clenched his teeth, forcing himself to stand. He lifted another rock, nearly stumbling under its mass. He threw it, his arm tearing with effort. It hit low, but it hit. He pulled another, and another, each one ripping at his strength. His body begged him to stop, but his heart would not.

At last the final stone struck high against the bark, splitting it in a sharp crack. Brak swayed on his feet, dizzy, his chest heaving like he had run for miles. His arms hung heavy at his sides, raw and weak.

Matto stepped closer. For a long moment he only looked at Brak, silent, the faintest glint in his eye. Then he laid a heavy hand on Brak's shoulder and grunted, *"Good."*

The word filled Brak more than food or rest. His chest swelled though his body shook. He straightened, pride burning hot in him. He had not failed. He had stood, he had lifted, he had thrown. He had made Matto nod.

The marks on the tree stood as proof, bark split and scarred, roots battered by stone. Brak gazed at them, his breath still fast, and felt something grow in him that had not been there before.

Matto turned back toward the ridge. He grunted, *"We go."*

Brak followed at once, his steps lighter despite the

soreness in his muscles. The forest closed around them again as they left the clearing, the marks of their training still fresh on the trees behind them. Brak's thoughts burned with fierce fire. For the first time in many days, the shame of failure dimmed. He had learned something new. He had made Matto nod. He had made him grunt good.

The stones still echoed in his ears, each strike a promise that he could be more than he was.

CHAPTER 31

Brak woke with his heart pounding. Rain hammered outside, a hard curtain that ate the edges of every sound. From far below came a dull crack, blurred by distance and water. Another followed, sharper but still wrapped in rain, like ice breaking under deep river.

He sat up, listening. Even with the storm, his ears caught the faint clatter of stone on wood, the low drum of weight on a roof. The echoes slid across the valley and up through the trees, softened by the downpour. He rose and moved toward the mouth of the cave, careful where his feet found the ground.

Cold air met him. Rain hissed through the trees and poured from the leaves in sheets. He angled through the trees toward the path that led to the ridge lip. The rocks were slick. Roots shone dark and wet. He kept low, breath steaming, hands brushing trunks to feel his way.

At the ridge he crouched and peered into the valley. Through the rain the hairless ones' dwelling showed as broken angles, soft lights inside. Four tall shapes moved against the walls. The juveniles. Their arms rose and fell. He heard glass yield, a dull shiver under the rain's steady roar. Light jumped within the rooms. Another window broke. Rain poured into the open square and ran in bright threads down the siding.

They would go in next. He knew it. The hairless ones inside would have no walls left to hold. Brak's chest tightened. He thought of Kara's sideways look and of Matto's heavy quiet, the rules set for him like stones on a path. If he moved now he would bring their anger; if he stayed still, the breaking would be on him. He glanced toward the cave, a quick flash of guilt, and held to the ridge, rain running off his brow, watching for the one clean moment to act.

****

The storm came hard just after midnight, rain beating the roof until the house seemed to breathe with it. Alice lay awake, listening to the steady rush, the gutters overflowing, the wide sheets slapping off the eaves. John snored once and rolled. The bedside clock gave off a weak glow. After the last time, they had left boards over several frames, telling themselves it was only until things calmed.

Something cracked on the far side of the house, faint as if underwater, a hollow drum from a boarded window. Alice held her breath. A sharper crack came closer. Not branches. Not hail. Glass.

She sat up fast and grabbed John's shoulder. "John, wake up."

He blinked into the dim room. "What is it?"

"They're back."

"Ah. Dammit," he said under his breath.

The rain drowned most of it, but a thin rattle filtered through. Stone on siding. Another crack. A window surrendered with a brittle shiver. In the rooms with boards, the blows thudded and held.

John was on his feet, awake all at once. "Stay down," he whispered. "Stay away from the windows."

****

Brak saw a hand rake out shards from a low window. From inside the dwelling, a loud bang cracked the air. The juvenile at the window recoiled with a scream and ran from the wall, clutching its hand.

Brak dropped two quarters down the slope to a shelf of scrub and wet rock. He'd had enough of watching.

He set his feet in the stance Matto had taught him: front foot planted, hips coiled, shoulder up, off hand loose to guide.

He hurled a stone hard and flat and clipped one of the four at the shoulder. Another throw smacked the mud only inches from a foot. He threw again and caught a thigh. Three of the sasquatch below jerked their heads uphill and charged the slope.

****

Alice grabbed John's arm. "Now," she whispered. John raised the rifle and fired. The shot cracked through the room, the rain swallowing the echo. The hand jerked back from the frame with a raw scream, blood spattering the shards. Heavy steps stumbled away from the house. Alice saw shadows outside turn uphill as if pulled by a wire. Three shapes broke into a run toward the slope. The other one stayed by the barn and held its arm to its chest.

Maybe they're leaving, she thought to herself.

****

Brak saw them coming and steadied his breathing. He reset and sent a flat stone at the lead. It struck above the brow with a hard crack and the runner stumbled to a knee, but the other two reached him. Hands took his arms as they hauled Brak down the slope, through brush and wet trunks, breath hot on his neck. As they approached the barn, Brak twisted, threw an elbow, tore loose for a heartbeat, then a forearm caught his back and shoved him forward. A knee drove into his ribs. A fist clipped his cheek. He snarled and raked for eyes.

The roar came like a tree splitting, deep and full enough

to make the rain seem to pause. The two on Brak flinched and looked up through the branches as Matto burst from the dark, sprinting, roaring.

Matto reached them in a split second and hit like falling rock. One juvenile tumbled head over fist, leaving a trail in the churned mud. Another slammed into a fence post at the edge of the trees hard enough to rattle the rails. Matto seized a third by the nape and lifted, skin bunching under his hand, rain webbing between his fingers. He hurled it across the yard into the fire pit.

The fourth leapt for Matto's ribs and raked long lines down his side. Matto turned and drove a fist into its chest. Wet knuckles thudded on bone. The juvenile dropped, gasping for breath.

Brak staggered up, lungs burning. The storm blurred the edges of everything. Two juveniles rushed Matto from opposite sides. A third slid low toward Brak, hands spread, trying to bring him down again. Brak stepped back and let it overreach, then drove his forehead into its face. He felt teeth go. The juvenile reeled, blood washing into the rain. Matto took one on the shoulder and threw it into the barn wall. The boards boomed and dropped a trickle of dust. Far inside, something small scuttled and went still.

Another juvenile climbed the fence rail and sprang for Matto's back. Brak's hand closed on a stone half-buried in the wet. He set his feet where the mud would hold. He lifted his arm and snapped.

The rock struck the springer's mouth with a hard wet sound. Blood and water mixed and flew. The body turned off course and crashed down hard in the mud, choking.

Matto's eyes cut to Brak. He grunted, *"Good."*

Heat ran through Brak's chest. He grabbed another stone from the churned ground.

The broken-mouthed juvenile pushed up on shaking hands and spat red into the rain.

He grunted, *"Kill both."*

He rushed. Matto stepped into him, but the one behind Matto clamped both arms around his waist and heaved, a foolish try against an older, taller, heavier body. Mud slid. Matto bent his knees and rooted. The third circled for Brak, hands low and fast.

Brak threw at the circling one. The stone clipped his shoulder and made him flinch. He hurled another at the spine of the one gripping Matto. The wet thud loosened the hold for a breath. Matto broke free, turned, and drove his knee up into the second's jaw. Teeth cracked like small stones under weight.

The second fell and writhed, clutching his mouth. The other two regrouped in the rain, faces twisted by pain and fury. The storm beat down, making rivers along the rails, turning the yard to slick clay.

They changed tactics. One scooped a double handful of small stones and flung them. Matto turned his head and took the grit across his shoulder. Brak shut his eyes and felt one bite his brow. He blinked through the sting and saw the third lift a rock two hands high for the back of Matto's skull.

Brak ran and knew he would not make it. He snatched a flat heavy stone from the muck and hurled it ugly, arm tired and burning. The weight carried it true. It hit the raised forearm and knocked it aside. The killing blow fell to the sodden ground and cut only mud.

Matto's hands closed on the thrower's shoulders. He drove him into the barn wall and the juvenile broke through the wooden panels, boards thundering as he crashed to the dirt inside and lay winded.

Shame took them where pain had not. They scrambled

up, dragging the worst hurt. One looked past Matto at Brak and pointed with a shaking hand.

He chattered, *"Leader will know. He come. That ridge is ours."*

Another spat blood in a thin line that rain tore away.

He grunted, *"You will end for this."*

They took off for the far trees and vanished into the wet dark, low growls trailing and drowned by the storm. Silence took shape in the rain. Water ran from the barn eaves in steady ropes. Mud held the prints of heavy feet, some deep, some smeared. Far off, the dwelling glowed with one small light and the rest dark.

Matto breathed deep and slow. He turned to Brak and looked him over, rain streaking the blood from Brak's brow. He touched the cut with two fingers and drew his hand away.

He grunted, *"You hurt."*

Brak shook his head. He replied, *"Not bad."*

Matto looked to the trees where the four had gone. He sniffed.

Even through rain, another scent rode the wind far off.

His eyes narrowed as he grunted, *"The other clan."*

Brak swallowed and chattered, *"They will come for us, won't they?*

Matto turned as he grunted, *"Soon."*

****

Footsteps beat the yard, then moved away, some pounding up the slope toward the ridge before turning back through the trees. Over the rain came voices, quick and layered, too fast to catch, a rush of harsh syllables that sounded like a foreign tongue. The blows were not at the house now but somewhere between the ridge and the barn. The voices rose and tangled with the slap of bodies in the mud, and a massive roar lifted over the storm.

"Do you hear that?" Alice whispered.

John nodded, eyes fixed on the side door. "They're out by the barn."

They edged to the mudroom doorway and crouched low, keeping to the dark. Through the rain and the smear of the yard they could make out shapes near the barn and the fence rails. Two figures moved together against four. One was massive, shoulders like a wall. The other was smaller, quick in the mud, stones flashing from its hand in hard arcs.

Alice stared, breath shallow. "John," she said, barely a sound. "The small one. I think that's the one I saw at the creek. It looks different from the other ones."

Another roar rolled across the yard, deep enough to shake the frames that were left and drum the boards still on the windows. The barn boomed, a long shudder running through it. Something slammed a fence rail and broke it with a crack.

A choked scream cut short, then only rain again for a breath.

They slid back from the doorway, hearts racing.

The sounds slowed. Footsteps dragged. A low growl faded toward the tree line. The rain filled the spaces where the other sounds had been.

They waited, frozen, counting breaths.

The kitchen lay in dim gray. The window above the sink was gone, the frame torn, the curtains stuck to the counter in wet folds. No shapes moved. Only the storm.

John met Alice's eyes and kept his voice low. "Let's just stay right here, for now."

He pulled her in with one arm and held her, the rifle in his other hand, muzzle down.

Alice nodded, her throat too tight for words. She rested her head on his chest and listened to the rain soak the house. Her mind tried to run, first to anger, then to the fear that had been eating her for months. She thought of the young one by the creek and the axe propped on the porch after. Good and bad.

Both true at once. She could not make sense of it.

****

They moved into the trees and began the climb. Mud pulled at them.

They reached the path near the cave just as Kara came up through the trees, carrying a deer over her shoulder, rain flattening her hair to her shoulders. She stopped when she saw the blood on Brak and the claw lines along Matto's ribs.

She grunted, *"You went."*

Brak dropped his gaze. He grunted, *"Yes."*

She looked from him to Matto, breath quick. She chattered, *"What happen."*

Matto kept walking. He grunted, *"Later."*

They reached the cave. Water dripped from the stone lip in a steady thread. Kara pulled the deer just inside the mouth. She cleaned Brak's brow with soft moss and pressed more against Matto's cuts. Brak sat near the entrance and watched the rain blur the sky while Matto and Kara ate.

Deep in the trees on the other side of the valley, a long call rose above the storm. It was not coyote. Not wolf. It climbed and held and dropped to a low grind that lifted the hair along Brak's arms.

Kara flinched. She looked at Matto, eyes wide.

He grunted, *"Leader."*

They did not sleep. Dawn came slow and gray through rain. When the light reached the rock, Matto stood and watched the valley from a ledge on the ridge. He said nothing. Brak knew what sat in him. Kara knew too. They would not run. Not yet.

****

John followed Alice to the hall cupboard and helped pull out towels to soak the water creeping across the floor. She was turning back when another sound rose outside, not the shrieking of the smaller ones, but a low call from far off, long and steady and old.

It slid under the storm and into the walls. It made her teeth hurt.

John whispered, "What the hell?"

She shook her head. She did not know. She only knew it made the house feel smaller.

After a long while the front room lights flickered. John risked a step from the hallway and turned off every switch he could reach. Darkness came back, soft and wet, with the small light of the microwave clock the only glow left.

"Sit," he said. "Breathe."

They sat on the kitchen floor, backs against cabinets, water ticking around them. They did not speak. The storm worked at the broken places. Somewhere deep in the house a small alarm chirped and died.

Much later, when the rain eased, they moved room to room with a flashlight, stepping around glass, turning off anything still humming. The damage was worse than the last time. Windows gone. Water everywhere. On the boarded frames the planks were gouged and loosened but had held. On the ground outside they saw stones shining clean with rain. Fence rails split. Mud churned with deep tracks headed toward the trees.

Alice stood in the living room and listened to the quiet under the storm's last hiss. She felt empty and shaking. She looked at John and saw his jaw set hard, his eyes shadowed.

"Why are they doing this?" she said.

He did not answer. He looked out through the open square where the window had been.

"We board it up at first light," he said. "We're not staying here another night."

CHAPTER 32

The storm burned itself down to a steady drip, as Alice and John watched the dark lighten by inches. When the sun finally lifted somewhere behind the low clouds, John pulled on his boots and jacket and said nothing. Alice was already dressed. They stepped out onto the porch and took in the glass scattered like ice, the wet curtains stuck to the floor, the fence rail split, the churned mud. The quiet felt thin, like it could tear if they breathed too hard.

They went room to room with towels and mopped up the standing water. They wrung the towels into buckets and poured them out on the gravel. When the floors stopped shining, they laid dry towels where the leaks still tapped, then looked at each other and nodded. It was enough for now.

They got in the truck. John eased them down the long driveway, careful around ruts and soft spots. The first ten miles into town were gravel, the tires humming over washboard and stones, dust rising and hanging under the low sky. The clouds held, but the rain had stopped. Neither spoke.

The gravel gave way to old asphalt that lifted and dipped through pasture and timber. The sky hung low. In places a thin ground fog curled over the ditches. They passed three cars in all. A rancher with a stock trailer. A county truck with a flashing light. A woman in a sedan who kept her eyes forward.

Alice kept her hands folded tight in her lap. She thought of the hand coming through the window. Her throat went dry, and a shiver went up her spine. She swallowed and looked out at the gray fields. A hawk lifted off a fence post and drifted low along the ditch, watching the ground.

At the edge of town the hardware store sat in a squat block of cinder and tin, paint weathered down to a flat red. John pulled in under the awning where stacks of plywood were stored. He turned off the engine and listened to the quiet hum of the building, the click of hot metal on the hood cooling.

Inside, the store smelled like cut wood and machine oil. The clerk at the counter nodded once and went back to a receipt book. John and Alice walked the aisles without words. They picked heavy sheets of plywood, thicker than they needed, and a box of long screws. John added a hand saw and two more pry bars. Alice grabbed a pair of gloves and a handful of shop towels. They met at the register and paid. The clerk helped them load, sliding the sheets onto the truck bed. John tied the stack down and tugged the rope twice.

They climbed back in and pulled out toward home. The weight of the wood changed the way the truck sat on the springs. The sky had not lifted. They drove in silence for a while, the road ticking under the tires.

Three miles from town John spoke.

"We should go," he said. "For a while."

Alice turned to him, then back to the road. "Where."

"Seattle," he said. "We stay with Claire. Three weeks. Maybe four. See if it dies down. Gives us time to think of better options."

Alice watched the center line roll under them. "I can pack today," she said. "We can leave this afternoon."

He nodded, jaw tight. "We board the windows, lock what we can, and go."

She sat with it for a few beats. Relief came first, light and quick, and she felt guilty for it. Then the worry came in behind it, bigger. "She will ask why," Alice said.

"I know," John said. "We keep it simple."

Alice nodded. "I will call her when we get home."

They drove past a stand of cottonwoods, their trunks dark with old rain. Water still ran in threads at the edges of the fields. A line of black cattle stood along a fence, heads down, tails switching. Beyond them the hills lifted, pale with soaked grass and old snow in the cuts.

"I hate leaving," Alice said. "I hate it."

"So do I," John said.

"We will come back," she said.

"Yup," he said, and he made it sound like a fact.

The miles fell away. The road rose and smoothed out along the ridge above their place. The clouds began to thin but did not break. Far off, the mountains were only shapes behind the gray. Alice felt the knot in her chest tighten again as the trees they knew came into view. The driveway turned off and dropped toward the house.

They pulled up and sat for a moment, looking at what the night had done. It was so much worse in the daylight. The living room gaped at them. The dining room window was a torn mouth. The kitchen window above the sink was gone to the frame. The porch sagged a little where a post had cracked. The barn door hung crooked, one roller off its track.

"Let's get to it," John said.

They carried the sheets to the porch and set them in pairs against the wall. John measured by eye and cut, the saw leaving clean edges. Alice held the panels in place while he drove screws until the drill's clutch clicked hard. They moved from room to room, working without talk, pausing only to haul out wet curtains and lay fresh towels where drips still fell. The hours went by in gray light. The house looked smaller and tighter with each window covered.

When they finished the last one, John stood back and set his hands on his hips. "It will hold," he said. "For now."

Alice nodded. "I will pack," she said.

He checked his watch. "I will load the truck. Food, coats, blankets."

She looked at him. "And then."

"And then we go," he said. "We can make Spokane by evening."

She pictured the long road west, the passes, the big dark water beyond. She pictured Claire's small house and the way it smelled like coffee and soap. She felt the relief again, and then the guilt for feeling it when the place they loved stood hurt in front of her.

"Okay," she said.

They moved through the house one more time, checking doors and the garage. In the kitchen Alice paused and listened. The leaks had slowed to a faint tap into a bowl she had set below. The sound was steady. She let it count a few beats for her. Then she shut off the last light and followed John out.

They loaded the suitcases into the truck and climbed in. The boards over the windows looked like a promise and a wound at the same time. John started the engine. Alice set her phone in her lap and pulled up Claire's number.

"I will tell her we are coming," she said.

"Okay. Remember to keep it simple," John said.

He pulled the truck around and started up the driveway.

The house slipped behind the trees again. Alice watched it for as long as she could, then faced forward and held onto the thought that they would come back, that the place would be here when the nights quieted, that there would be time to find better choices than fear.

CHAPTER 33

Days slid by after the fight, the rain shouldering east until a hard washed blue settled over the sky. The cave held them in its dark fold of stone, where every small sound seemed too loud: a pebble shifting, a breath changing, the thin tick of water seeping from a crack and dropping to the floor. Matto and Kara stayed near the cave, especially when they hunted.

Matto listened to it all and kept his face still. He had wondered, more than once, if they should leave. He looked out at the valley and thought of the long miles behind them, the storms, the hunger, the river that had tried to take them. He counted what this place gave. Deer on the ridges. Rabbits in the brush. Grouse in the lower pines. Water not far. A cave that held them well enough. He weighed it against the scent on the dawn and dusk wind, the old heavy smell that meant the other clan, aware of them now, checked this ground from time to time. He felt stubborn heat move through his chest. Why leave ground that fed them. Why climb back into emptiness. The hairless ones would not scale the ridge. Their paths were wrong for such climbs. Only the other clan was a true threat. He had tried not to be part of their games. He had warned Brak to stay out. Yet he knew the fight by the barn would pull a string that led to a hand. The hand would belong to a leader.

Brak kept to the cave for most of those days. His body ached in deep places. His thigh still held a dull numb spot where a kick had landed. His throwing arm throbbed if he lifted it too fast. Shame lay on him when he woke and before he slept. He did not speak of it. He sat near the mouth and watched the light move across the stone and the trunks below. When he rose, Kara's eyes found him at once and pushed him back to the bedding with only a look. Matto said little, but his silence had weight. Brak did not mind the rules. He needed the stillness. He needed the ache to settle. Yet the nag of what was right gnawed at him like a small, hard-tooth animal, never quite stopping, even when he slept.

Kara moved in quiet patterns. She smoothed the bedding, checked old wrappings, found fresh resin, and laid more boughs where the floor chilled. She stepped out for short turns to fetch needles and dry grass and returned before the sun shifted. She watched Brak when he thought she did not. She watched Matto when he stood too long at the lip and stared down into the trees.

Birds moved differently. At dawn they sang, and then they did not. The far wood knocks came and went in threes, then in fives, then in a single hard strike as if to say enough. Twice Matto found stones stacked near a trail that climbed toward their cave. Small piles, not of river shape. Once he found a pine gouged high where only strong arms could reach. He said nothing. He brushed the piles flat with his foot. He marked one of their own trees in return, a slow rip that laid pale wood bare, then left the strip hanging like a tongue. The message was simple. We are here.

The second evening, wind from the west drew the scent of the other clan up the gullies and set it into the cave mouth like a slow, cold hand. Brak lifted his head at once. Matto already stood. Kara set her work down and went still. The scent did not pass. It held.

Matto walked out of the cave and stood at the mouth, as Kara and Brak followed. A shape formed at the lower bend of the path. Not the leader. A messenger. Older female by the look of the hair that hung in wet ropes. Broad through the shoulders. Scar down one forearm. She lifted a limbless branch and struck the stone. Three clean knocks rang out. She lowered the branch and chattered low, the words plain, the tone hard.

She chattered, *"Leader calls. Two falls of sun. Low clearing by water. Come. Speak. Or we come. We take."*

She turned and was gone. The scent drifted after her, then thinned.

Kara let out the breath she had been holding. She looked at Matto. Brak watched them both, worried at what he had brought down upon them.

Matto did not move. His eyes were on the place where the messenger had stood. He said nothing for a long while. At last he turned back into the cave and sat.

Kara followed him. Her voice came low, careful.

She chattered, *"We go?"*

Matto's jaw worked once. He grunted, *"Wait."*

That night the cave breathed slow and shallow. Wind ran the ridge and made the pines sing one note without tune. Brak lay awake and stared at the dark above him. He thought of the messenger's words. *Come. Speak. Or we come.* He felt small and hot at the same time. He had brought eyes onto them. He knew this. He would carry it if he had to. He turned once on the bedding and winced at the pain in his side. He slept without rest.

****

Morning broke thin and cold. The sky held a white film like shed skin stretched across it. Matto rose without a sound and left. He moved along the ridge away from the cave and down into the trees. He returned before noon with a grouse and two rabbits hanging from one hand, his other hand wet where he had drank from the stream. He ate little. He handed more to Brak than to himself. Kara watched and said nothing.

On the third day after the fight, the birds stilled at midmorning and did not start again. The wind went slack. Sound carried too well. Far down in the valley a wood knock fell like a dropped stone. Then another answered from a slope closer to them. Matto stood at the cave mouth and did not step out. He waited.

Footfalls climbed, not hidden, not fast. The messenger returned. She stopped where she had before and set the clean end of the branch to the ground. Her eyes fixed on Matto. Brak felt his skin tighten. Kara's breath went small.

The messenger chattered, *"Leader waits. Sun drops. River bend. Come now. Or we come here."*

Matto did not answer at once. He looked at Brak and Kara. He chattered, *"If I not return, you leave. Straight away. They come and end you both."* He gave a small nod, and then turned around.

Matto stepped from the cave mouth and walked down to the bend in the path. The older female turned and led the way. He went with her into the trees and was gone.

CHAPTER 34

The path eventually came out of the trees and ran along a high rim above a lake. A narrow strip of forest clung to the edge. Beyond it the ground dropped in a low bluff to a bed of rounded boulders, and beyond the stones the water lay dark and smooth. Wind crossed the open and brought the lake's cold skin to land. Pine gave way to alder and willow. The ground was packed with old tracks, some filled with water, some dried to cracked cups.

Matto stepped from the shade and stopped at the edge above the drop. He stood alone. His chest rose slow. He counted what the ridge gave and what it would take. He weighed the two behind him against the cost ahead. No tremor lived in him, only the want to finish it and be done. If the price for holding ground was his blood, he would pay it, so long as Kara and Brak were spared.

He watched as shapes slid from the trees around the bend and took their places. One. Five. Ten. More. They formed a wide half circle that left the water and the drop to stone at Matto's back. Twenty at least. All eyes on him. Some were young, some old, males and females. The leader had chosen this open place where the ground held no one's scent for long.

At the center stood two. One was tall and heavy through the chest, the hair along his arms darker than the rest, his jaw square, his stance easy in the way of those who do not have to prove what they are. His name was Ruk. The other's hair was silvered at the cheeks and brows, his ribs narrow, his eyes calm and deep. Around them, the clan shifted and went still again, the sound of many lungs breathing out.

Ruk stepped forward a pace. His stare did not waver. He lifted his chin and grunted, *"You."*

Matto said nothing. The lake wind made the short hair along his forearms stir like grass.

Ruk pointed with a slow hand toward the trees beyond the bend, toward the valley where the dwelling sat.

He grunted, *"You hurt young ones."*

Matto held his gaze. He replied, *"Yes."*

A low murmur ran the circle, not words, only breath turning to sound. A few bared their teeth. A few hands curled. Ruk took another half pace. He grunted, *"Why."*

Matto drew a breath and let it out. He set his feet deeper into the sand and gave the words the shape they needed.

He chattered, *"My small one watched your four. Night after night. He saw them throw at hairless ones. Break walls. Climb. Hunt fear. I told him turn away. I told him leave hairless ones. He thinks right is not a thing to turn from. He is young. He sees straight. I know this. I also know when we show, no end is clean. Hairless ones bring more, and more, until all is fire and noise. So I told him no. He went anyway. I came."*

Ruk listened with his head a little to the side, like a wolf testing wind.

He grunted, *"You come for hairless ones."*

Matto shook his head once.

He chattered, *"I come to pull my small one back. I come to end your four's play on that den. I come to make quiet."*

Ruk's nostrils flared. He turned his head and looked along his own line as if counting. He faced Matto again.

He grunted, *"You come here. To our land."*

Matto's shoulders lifted and fell. *"We walk long. We lose much. We do not want fight. We take nothing. We break nothing. We stay on ridge. We eat and sleep. We keep to ourselves. We come in peace. We want no trouble with hairless ones. We want to be left alone. We leave all alone."*

A few in the circle shifted. One old female nearest the water set her weight to one hip and watched Matto with something like interest. Others chuffed but did not speak.

Ruk's mouth went flat.

He looked out across the lake and trees and chattered, *"This is ours."*

Matto did not blink.

He chattered, *"You say this. I say I do not fight for empty words. I fight if my small one is taken. I fight if you climb my cave. I do not fight to draw lines in dirt."*

Ruk's jaw moved once. He lifted his hand and pointed at Matto's chest again.

He grunted, *"You hurt our four."*

Matto's voice stayed slow, the words even.

He chattered, *"After warning given. After my small one was blooded and dropped and kicked. After that, yes, I broke them. Enough to stop. Harass hairless ones again, it end in blood for all."*

A thick-shouldered male to the right let out a low rumble. Another cracked his knuckles against his own palm. The half circle leaned in without moving their feet.

Ruk grunted, *"Does not matter. Ours. You go. Or die."*

Matto felt the air along his back where the water waited and the drop to the stones began. He did not turn to it. He did not look at the trees behind the line. He did not look for help that was not there.

He grunted, *"We do not go."*

Ruk's lips peeled from his teeth without sound. He drove his right fist into the earth at his feet. Dirt and grass leapt. The ground shivered.

On Ruk's left, the silver-haired one raised a hand without haste. His eyes were on Matto, not on the fist. He had not moved since he took his place.

He grunted, *"Enough."*

All motion in the half circle stopped. Ruk did not look at the hand. He kept his head forward. The silver-haired one let his hand fall to his side. His voice came lighter than his chest suggested, steady and cold.

He chattered, *"New one is right on one thing. Do not go near hairless ones. Do not show. Do not break their walls. History says when we do, it brings blood. That is old truth."*

Ruk did not answer. The silver-haired one turned his head a sliver toward him without breaking his gaze on Matto.

He chattered, *"History says another thing. If you want a new one to leave, you fight. Leader to leader. All watch. One falls. One takes ground. No long war in trees. No slow bleed."*

Ruk's eyes slid to the silver-haired one and held, one breath, two. Then he looked back to Matto. His lips curled into something like a smile and did not reach his eyes.

He chattered, *"I end him too easy."*

With a stone face, Matto chattered, *"As it comes."*

A ripple went through the line as if a wind had passed that only they could feel. Knuckles flexed. Toes dug. The ground seemed to lean toward the space between the two.

Matto set his feet deeper. His face did not change. He could hear his own heart. He could taste the old iron smell of the elder, the wet bark scent of the young, the cold stone breath of the lake. He did not hear birds. He did not hear frogs. He heard only the space before a fall.

A young male two places down from Ruk lifted his chin and sniffed. His eyes went past Matto's shoulder, over Matto's back, into the trees beyond. He squinted, then barked a sharp sound and pointed.

He chattered, *"There. Show."*

Heads turned. A few took half steps as if to circle. Matto did not move. He knew the smell even before the shapes came. It reached him and made his teeth clench.

Kara stepped from the shade first, slow, her hands open and low. Brak came after, smaller, shoulders square though he trembled. They kept to the trail cut by many feet and walked until they stood where the line could see them but not close enough to touch.

Matto turned his head and gave them both his eyes. The look had weight.

He chattered, *"You should not have come."*

Kara did not drop her gaze. She drew a breath and gave the words without flinch.

She chattered, *"We had to."*

Brak met Matto's eyes. For the first time he saw something softer than anger and hate.

Across the half circle, Ruk let out a soft sound that was not a laugh and not a sigh. He tilted his head, taking them in, measuring, perhaps enjoying the way fear changes the taste of air.

He grunted, *"Good."*

He lifted his chin and let his voice carry. *"You watch. You see me end him."*

The wind came off the lake colder than before. The water darkened where clouds moved over the sun. Somewhere far away a raven called once and fell quiet. The ground between the two leaders seemed to rise. The clan did not breathe. The elder lowered his eyes to the sand and then up again to Matto. He said nothing more. The line tightened by inches.

The open space held like a drawn bow.

CHAPTER 35

Ruk's gaze slid past Matto to the two shapes at the trees. He bared his teeth and moved for Brak, fast and low, sand and grit lifting under his heels.

Matto reached him in three hard strides, caught his forearm, and slammed chest to chest. They locked and shoved, feet carving trenches. Ruk tried to rip free toward the small one. Kara stepped in front of Brak, shoulders set. Matto would not give. He bulled him sideways toward the shelves. Ruk twisted loose and chopped at Matto's neck. Matto ducked, drove his forehead into Ruk's chest, and walked him back two steps. The lake slapped stone below.

Brak tried to step around Kara until her hand clamped around his wrist.

She grunted, *"Stay."*

They traded short and brutal. Ruk's hooks drummed ribs. Matto answered with a grip that sank to bone and a knee that thudded thigh. Ruk feinted high and raked low, nails opening four lines across Matto's belly. Matto crowded him and swept behind the ankle. Ruk dropped, sprang up angry, and chopped again. The edge of a blow split Matto's brow. Blood ran hot into his right eye. The lid puffed at once. He blinked and the world on that side closed. His right eye swelled shut almost instantly.

Ruk smelled the change and pressed. He cuffed the ear, hammered the jaw, drove Matto toward the slick rocks. Matto set his feet and took it, head low, breath steady. Ruk burst sudden with both hands to the chest, a bull rush that gave no time.

Matto's heel skated on bare rock. The slick face let go. He slipped, turned, and vanished over the bluff. His back hit a ledge with a flat crack. His shoulder bent wrong under him. He flipped and struck the boulders below hard enough to shake loose rocks from the shelf. Even the clan's low sea of breathing went still. For a long heartbeat there was only the sound of water folding against stone and falling back again.

Brak tore free. He slid down the wet rock on hands and feet, nails scraping lichen, hip bumping hard. He reached the boulders and dropped to his knees beside Matto.

Matto lay twisted among the stones. One eye swollen shut. The other dull and wide. Blood crawled from his brow and along his cheek. His left shoulder sat wrong, the round of it flattened and low. Every breath was a hitch. His right palm was torn and sandy where he had tried to catch himself. He stared past Brak at nothing.

Brak pressed his palm to Matto's chest and felt a shallow beat.

He chattered, *"Up. Please. Up."*

Matto did not answer. His good eye fluttered and fixed on nothing.

Above, Ruk peered over the lip. He bared his teeth and heaved a river boulder into the cradle of his arms. He tested its weight, breath harsh. He began to climb down fast, fingers clawing cracks, the stone hugged to his chest. He found a ledge above Matto, set the boulder to his shoulder, and shifted to drop it clean onto Matto's head.

Brak put his forehead to Matto's and shook with it.

He chattered, *"Get up. Need you. Please."*

Matto's good eye found him through the blur. Something old sparked. The shadow of the boulder slid across them.

Ruk moved to let it fall.

Matto's hand shot out and caught Ruk's ankle. He wrenched. Balance went. The boulder lurched from Ruk's grip, struck the ledge, bounced, and rolled into the lake with a heavy plunge. Ruk pinwheeled for a heartbeat and dropped feet first. He hit the river stones, slid, and rose to hands and knees with the breath knocked out of him.

Matto rolled to a knee and rose with a sound from deep in his chest. He moved like a tree coming back from wind. His right eye was sealed. Blood crusted the lashes. His left shoulder hung and then shifted as he slammed it sideways into a low rock. A wet pop and a flash of pain. The joint slid home crooked but working. He staggered once and caught Ruk by the forearm and hair.

He dragged Ruk across the boulders, feet grinding wet stone, and hauled him to the waterline. He stepped into the lake to the knee. The cold bit through skin and bone. Ruk swung wild and clipped Matto's cheek. Matto did not stop. He poured his weight forward and forced Ruk back until the lake took his calves. He pressed his forearm across Ruk's throat and drove him under.

Bubbles rose and broke. Ruk thrashed. Water slapped Matto's chest and ran off in sheets. The half circle leaned as one, watching the fight. The elder did not blink.

Brak stood on the rocks, fists to his mouth, shaking. Kara steadied herself with a hand to the alder and did not look away.

Ruk bucked. The first heave almost broke the hold. The second did less. The third was weak and slow. Matto held him there, not crushing, holding that edge where a choice lives. He turned to look at the elder with his good eye, then at the line, then down at the dark water.

He grunted, *"Enough."*

He lifted his weight a finger's width. Ruk broke the surface and dragged air that scraped his throat. He coughed water, chest hitching, eyes wide and lost for a beat.

Matto kept him in the cold, forearm at the base of the neck, not the throat, his knee pinning one arm, the other trapped by the body's own weight. He held long enough that the choice could be seen by every eye on the shore.

He grunted, *"Live."*

The word fell and sank.

Ruk blinked up through wet hair. The hate in him

wavered. Something harder and cleaner sat under it. He spat a thin line of water and blood.

Matto stepped back and let the lake lift Ruk to his elbows. He moved away one pace, then another, still facing him. His chest heaved. Blood made maps on his skin. His right eye stayed sealed, a dark knot. Each breath pulled at a rib that had started to give. His left shoulder throbbed like fire.

Ruk rolled to his hands and knees and crawled a foot up the stones. He sat with his legs in the water, arms across his ribs, breath coming in quick saws. He did not look away.

Brak sagged and would have fallen if Kara had not caught his shoulder. He wiped his face with the back of his wrist and looked at Matto with something like thank you in his eyes. Kara's mouth was a hard line, but relief shook her once and then she was still again.

Matto did not raise his arms. He did not bare teeth. He stood with the cold on his legs, ready if Ruk twitched.

The clan did not speak. The elder watched with eyes that held no light and all of it. The shore seemed to wait with them, every leaf still.

CHAPTER 36

The clan held its half circle without a sound. Ruk sat in the wet sand, arm cradled, breath thin. Matto faced him, blood drying to a dark mask, his chest lifting slow.

The elder stepped to the lip before the rocks. He raised one hand, and the clan seemed to lean toward it.

He chattered, *"Fight ends. Law holds."*

He turned to Ruk first.

He chattered, *"Old truth stands. Do not go near hairless ones. Do not show. Do not break their walls."*

Ruk did not look at him. His eyes stayed on Matto, jaw set.

The elder faced Matto.

He chattered, *"Old law says one more. Leader to leader. One falls. Winner leads. Here. You win. You lead us. You three join this clan. One clan."*

Silence stretched. Wind slipped across the lake and came back colder. Matto looked to Kara and Brak. He met Kara's gaze. She nodded once, slow. He met Brak's. Brak nodded, small and absolute.

Matto turned back to the elder.

He grunted, *"I lead."*

He let the word sit and stood like stone.

Then he added, *"Hear me. No one goes to the hairless ones' dwelling. No throwing. No knocks at their walls. No showing. Cut marks in the tall pines from the bend to the ridge. That line holds. No feet cross toward the den of hairless ones without call. We keep quiet. We eat and sleep. We leave all alone."*

The messenger female stepped from the line and pointed downslope and up.

She chattered, *"Marks cut deep. From lake bend to ridge. This hold. We do not cross to their dwelling."*

Matto nodded once.

He grunted, *"Good."*

He looked to Ruk. The young leader's hair dripped lake water into the sand. His breath sawed thin. The hate in his eyes had shifted to something harder and cleaner.

Matto chattered, *"You stay. You keep law under me. You hold your four. If they break, you pay first."*

Ruk's nostrils flared. He swallowed once. He dipped his head the width of a finger.

He grunted, *"I hold."*

The elder walked down the rocks and touched the lake. He lifted water on his palm and let it fall to a flat river stone at his feet. He pressed his hand there, leaving a wet print. Then he dragged his nails across his own chest once, a thin line of blood, and set that blood to the same stone.

He chattered, *"Water hears. Stone remembers."*

He looked to Matto.

Matto stepped forward. He cut a short line on his forearm with a shard, pressed blood to the elder's mark, then set his wet palm to the lake and lifted it again. He did not flinch.

The female messenger raised the branch that had called them and struck a tree three times. The knocks rolled along the curve and across the lake.

The Elder chattered, *"Three knocks for peace. Break peace and there are no more knocks."*

The line held. No one spoke.

Across the clan, breaths went out together, rough and low. Heads dipped through the half circle, some quick, some slow. A few young ones stared at Ruk. He did not meet their eyes.

The elder turned to around and grunted, *"Done."*

He faced the line and walked from the water; the clan opened for him and closed behind. They slipped into alder and pine, feet leaving clean prints that filled with lake light. Ruk rose with help and went with them, head low, one arm tight to his chest.

Matto stood another long breath. The world tilted. Kara came under his bad shoulder without asking. Brak moved to the other side, small hand ready for what it could carry.

Matto grunted, *"I walk."*

Kara did not argue. She chattered, *"You walk. We steady."*

They left the clearing and climbed into the trees, following the other clan.

CHAPTER 37

The path climbed through alder and young pine, then angled along a slope where old needles made the ground slick. Matto walked with the elder beside him, Kara at his shoulder. Brak stayed tight to Kara's hip and watched the others' feet and hands, the way they set weight without haste.

Ruk came with them holding his ribs, one of his four steadying him by the elbow. He kept his eyes on the ground and placed each step clean.

They crossed a low rise where the wind turned, then dropped into a valley that did not show itself until they were inside it. Trees thickened as if grown to hide the bowl. The floor was moss and old grass. A creek wrote a thin silver line and slid under roots to small dark pools.

The elder lifted his chin toward the far wall. Rock shouldered out of the mountain there, brush braided tight across it. He turned toward a stand of young spruce, pushed through a narrow screen of deadfall, and the rock opened to a slim cleft no higher than a tall back and no wider than two shoulders. No slab. Only stone and shadow and the careful work of roots and time.

They turned sideways to pass. The seam bent once and drew back into a chamber not high but wide. A rib of stone ran along one side. A thin vent cut light along the roof and let the cave breathe.

The elder set his palm to the wall and knocked three times, slow and even. The sound went into the stone and came back soft.

He chattered, *"This is hold. This feeds. This hides."*

Matto listened to the cave talk to itself. He felt the weight above and the quiet underfoot. He met the elder's eyes, then set his own palm where the handprint darkened the wall.

He grunted, *"Good."*

The messenger female brought a bundle of boughs tied with vine and spread the needles along the stone rib. Two young males carried dry grass twisted into mats.

The elder touched the wall again.

He chattered, *"You three here. Six knocks for danger. Two then three for call."*

Matto nodded. He grunted, *"I hear."*

Kara and Brak stepped in together and looked around, their eyes moving over the rib of stone and the shadowed walls.

Matto turned to them both. For a moment he said nothing. Then he set his hand to Brak's shoulder and gave Kara his eyes.

He chattered, *"You see straight. Both of you. Keep that. Learn to lead with me. We make home here."*

Brak held his gaze and felt something warm in his chest he had not felt in a long time.

Kara looked at Brak, then back to Matto, the faintest lift at the corner of her mouth.

EPILOGUE

They came home in the pale light of a late afternoon, the truck rolling slow up the drive. New glass sat in the frames, clean putty bright along the edges. They hired a local handyman while they were gone. He set new glass in every frame and took the boards down. They told him it had been a bear. He didn't believe it.

The porch sagged a little at the cracked post. The barn door still hung off one roller. The place looked the same, and it did not. Nothing new was broken. Nothing had been moved. The quiet felt real and honest.

They walked through the rooms with care, opening two windows to let the house breathe again. Dust lifted in slanting sheets. Alice stood in the kitchen and touched the rim of the sink where the glass had once cut her finger. John moved a chair back to its old spot and swept a trail of grit into a pan. They did not say much. They were listening for a sound they remembered and did not want.

The first night passed and there were no rocks. No heavy feet thudding the porch. No monsters at the window. The second night was the same. By the end of the week they slept in shifts anyway, because habit had become a kind of safety, but the house held. By the end of the second week they slept at the same time, and the sleep was deep enough that they woke startled at the brightness of morning. When the wind came it was only wind. When a branch cracked it was only weight.

A month from the day they had left, they sat on the porch as the sun eased down through a rib of cloud. The sky went the soft color of apricots just before it fades. The grass in the yard had pushed up pale and then gone greener. Alice had set a potted geranium on the railing, its red brightening up the quiet house. John had the shotgun leaning against the wall beside him. He did not touch it. His hand rested on his knee, but his eyes kept measuring the tree line.

"Feels like it might hold," he said.

"Fingers crossed," Alice said.

She was looking at the yard where the shed sat in shadow,

its tin roof gone dull with spring dust. Something there moved. A shoulder, a change in light, a dark that was not the same dark as the wall behind it. She drew in a small breath and did not speak right away, because saying it would make it real.

John noticed the stillness in her. "What," he said.

Alice kept her voice low. "Look at the shed," she said.

They both watched. A shape slid out from the shadow and into the band of soft sun. It was the same one she had seen by the creek. Smaller than the ones that had come at night, not small in any normal sense, but young. The hair lay heavy and wet-looking along the arms and chest. The head was conical. The brow was low and heavy. He did not crouch or threaten. He stood with an odd calm, his face still.

He looked straight at them. Alice felt the same shock she had felt at the creek, but without the fear that had spiked then. The air around them seemed to thin and thicken at once.

"That is the same one," she said. "The one from the creek."

John's jaw worked and then settled. He started to reach for the gun and Alice told him no.

The young one knelt. He set something down on the bare ground where the grass had not come in yet. He did it slow, both hands, as if the thing were fragile. He stood again. He looked at them once more, a long look, head a little to the side. Then he turned and walked back behind the shed and was gone into the darker strip of trees without hurry.

John's hand found the shotgun and lifted it. He did not raise it. He laid it across his knees and looked at Alice.

"What did he leave," he said. "I hope it does not mean they are coming back to harass us."

They waited a few minutes because that felt like the right kind of careful. Birds started again in the tall spruce beyond the barn. The light fell another inch down the shed wall.

"Come on," Alice said as getting up.

They went together across the yard. John kept his eyes moving, sweeping the fence line, the gaps between trunks, the rise beyond the field. Alice stepped ahead when they reached the shed and knelt on the bare spot where the young one had put his hands. The ground was damp and cool. The thing sat there in a small ring of dust as if it had been waiting under the soil for a long time and had been lifted out whole.

It was a single agate with a geode-like formation, no

larger than her palm and heavy for its size. The outside was rough and dull, the color of old bone. A seam had opened along one curve. Inside, light lived. Bands of smoke and honey circled a small hollow where crystals had grown, tiny points that caught the last sun and held it like a secret. She turned it. The bands shifted. The heart of it changed from deep to pale and back again.

John kept his head on a swivel, then glanced over. "What is it?"

"A gift," she said softly.

Alice felt the cool of the stone in her hand and the odd warmth of the hollow where the points lay close together. She stood and held it so the light could find it. It flashed once and then went quiet in the shade of her fingers.

She looked at John. He met her eyes and then looked past her to the line of trees where the young one had vanished. He set the shotgun barrel down and let it rest on his boot. "I get the feeling we will not have any more trouble, John," she said. "That sasquatch is different."

THE END.

ABOUT THE AUTHOR

 Luka T. Jacobs, an author from the picturesque Illawarra region south of Sydney, Australia, is passionate about cryptids like Sasquatch and Dogman. She lives there with her partner and their dog, Finnigan.

Luka's love for animals and adventure fuels her storytelling. With a background in Graphic Design and Art, she adds a unique visual flair to her work. An avid traveler and explorer, she draws inspiration from the wild, eager to share her imaginative worlds with readers.

Luka T. Jacobs

Stay connected! *Follow me on **Facebook** and sign up for my **newsletter** to get the latest books, exclusive extras, and all things cryptid.*

FB: https://www.facebook.com/lukatjacobs
A: https://amazon.com/author/lukatjacobs
W: http://www.LukaTJacobs.com

JOIN CRYPTID HORROR CENTRAL

Join my email list and get first access to new releases and download my **FREE** short story *"The Dogman of Coldwater Creek"*.

WWW.LUKATJACOBS.COM

Dear Reader,

Thank you for diving into my book amidst a sea of choices, it truly means the world to me.

If you enjoyed the story, I'd love it if you shared your experience with others and left a review. As an independent author, your voice helps bring these tales to life for more readers, and every recommendation makes a tremendous impact.

Thank you again for joining me on this journey.
I'm so grateful to have you as a reader!

SNEAK PEAK:
SAVAGE ROGUE:
A NICOLE BERETTI THRILLER

Crack.

A sharp snap echoed through the dense Wyoming underbrush, but Tucker and Bo barely registered it as they trudged forward, their boots sinking into the damp forest floor. Shotguns hung from their shoulders, swinging slightly with each step as they moved in tandem. The sun's first light crept slowly over the horizon, slicing through the thick morning fog that clung low to the ground, casting an eerie glow over the wilderness.

Both men, rugged and in their early thirties, were marked by a long history of poor decisions and run-ins with the law. This morning was no different. They'd spent months running an illegal trapping operation, specifically targeting grizzly bears for their lucrative pelts. Their greed dulled any caution they might have felt about their scheme's dangers. The payday was all that mattered, enough to keep them going, no matter the risk or the rules they had to break.

"Man, I'm telling ya, this is it. If we succeed in trapping another grizzly, we'll be all set for the whole winter," Bo exclaimed, his voice hoarse from years of tobacco addiction. He hocked a loogie onto the dirt and fixed his grimy baseball hat.

"It better be worth it, that's all I'm saying. Ain't no way I'm freezin' my ass off for nothin'," Tucker grumbled, pulling his jacket tighter against the cold. He was thinner and shorter than Bo, his eyes darting nervously around the forest, always on the lookout. He knew they'd be in trouble if the game wardens caught them.

A few days ago, they set up a large bear trap hidden in the forest. Made of heavy-duty steel, the contraption was designed to trap anything that ventured onto the game trails. Bo purchased it from a dubious out-of-state source, boasting that no creature could escape once its jaws closed.

"Damn thing's strong enough to catch a tank," Bo had said when they set it. "Ain't no bear getting outta this one."

The trap had been carefully set along a narrow game trail, hidden just off a small clearing where animals often ventured through. They'd chosen the location to catch an unsuspecting grizzly on its routine path, banking on the season's chill to drive it along established trails. The payout for a full bear hide, they figured, would be worth all the freezing mornings, and the constant fear of getting nabbed by Fish and Game wardens.

Tucker kicked at a patch of dirt as they neared the clearing where the trap was set. "Think we got one?"

"If we did, it ain't goin' nowhere. This trap'll hold," Bo said, slapping Tucker on the back.

As they entered the clearing, both men suddenly stopped. Something big was caught in the trap.

"What the hell...?" Tucker said, squinting through the misty dawn light.

A huge creature, bigger than any bear they had ever witnessed, lay partially slouched on the forest ground. At first glance, they thought it might be a wolf, but as their eyes adjusted, it was clear this was no ordinary wolf. The creature was massive, measuring well over six feet in length, covered in thick, tangled fur, and possessed a formidable physique that resembled a creature from a nightmare rather than a real animal.

Its leg was ensnared in the steel jaws of the bear trap, the metal teeth piercing flesh and fur. The ground around the trap was covered in blood, dark and sticky in the faint light, and the soil indicated a struggle had occurred. The beast had clearly fought to free itself. The area around the trap was churned up, deep claw imprints etched into the earth where the creature had thrashed and tried to escape.

"Holy hell…" Bo whispered, stepping forward cautiously. "We… we got somethin' big. The boss is gonna love it!"

Tucker's stomach churned at the sight. "I-Is it… is it d-dead?"

Bo grinned. "Sure looks like it.

"Look at the trap," Tucker said, his voice trembling slightly. "Thing put up one hell of a fight."

Bo chuckled and approached the creature without hesitation. "Thing's as good as dead. Hell, it ain't movin' at all." He stood right next to its side, eyes gleaming with greed, and gave it a sharp kick to the ribs.

Tucker squinted, feeling a pit form in his stomach as he took in the massive, slumped form on the ground. "What… what the hell is that?"

Bo chuckled and stepped forward without hesitation. "This, my friend, is one huge freakin' wolf. The boss is gonna pay us big-time for this." His eyes lit up as he admired the creature's massive limbs and thick fur. "I woke up with a good feeling about today."

Tucker hesitated, casting a wary glance left and right, his nerves prickling as he took in the creature's massive form. "That... that ain't a normal wolf, Bo. It's too big. Looks like a freakin' werewolf or somethin'." His voice dropped to a whisper. "Maybe we should just leave it. Somethin' about this don't feel right, I tell ya."

Bo laughed, brushing off Tucker's concern. "What are you scared of, Tuck? This thing's our payday, and it's not even breathin'." He nudged the creature's side with his boot, his grin widening. "It's dead, see?"

Tucker's gut twisted, but he stayed silent, glancing around the clearing. The thick mist clung to the air, as the hairs on his neck bristled. "Alright... let's make it quick," he said, looking away from the creature's enormous form.

Bo knelt down beside the trap, his fingers fumbling with the latch. "Tucker, give me a hand with this," he said. Together, they pried the trap open, and with a metallic click, the jaws sprang apart, freeing the creature's leg.

For a moment, silence hung heavy in the air.

Then, in a sudden, terrifying blur, something exploded

from the shadows, a dark, hulking figure hurtling out of the trees with the speed and force of a freight train. Tucker barely registered what was happening before the creature was upon them, claws flashing in the dim light.

Bo's scream was short-lived as the creature's claws tore through his side, ripping through muscle and bone with ease. Blood sprayed across the clearing, splattering Tucker's face as he stumbled back, frozen in horror. Bo's eyes widened in shock, his hands clutching at the gaping wound in his chest as he staggered, his mouth opening in a silent scream.

The creature didn't hesitate. It lunged at Bo, driving him to the ground with bone-crushing force, its jaws closing around his throat. With a sickening crunch, its teeth tore through flesh, tendons and muscle, severing his spinal column in a single, brutal motion. Blood pooled beneath him, soaking into the dirt as his body went still, his lifeless eyes staring at the misty sky above.

"Oh, God... oh, Jesus Christ!" Tucker stammered, his body shaking as he stumbled backward, his gaze locked on the creature that now turned its attention toward him.

The beast loomed, massive and unnatural, its muzzle dripping with blood. beneath its dense fur as it stood there, staring down at Bo's mangled body with eyes that burned with a terrifying, almost human rage.

Tucker stared, transfixed, as it rose slowly onto two legs, towering over him, its broad shoulders heaving with every breath. The creature's eyes locked onto him, sharp and intelligent, gleaming with a hunger that turned his blood to ice.

Tucker felt the scream clawing its way up his throat, his mind urging him to run, but his legs were leaden, frozen by terror. The shotgun strapped across his shoulder was all but forgotten, dead weight in the haze of fear clouding his mind.

Then, with a low, guttural growl that reverberated in his chest, the beast lunged, closing the distance in a heartbeat. Its jaws clamped down on his arm, bone crunching beneath the brutal force, and in a single, terrifying wrench, it tore his arm clean off. A white-hot pain exploded through him as his scream shattered the morning silence, echoing through the trees while blood sprayed from the wound, staining the earth.

Tucker staggered backward, clutching at the raw, bleeding stump, his vision blurring as his strength ebbed with every heartbeat. His breaths came in shallow, panicked gasps as he stumbled through the underbrush, leaving a crimson trail in his wake.

But the beast wasn't finished.

With frightening speed, it lunged again, slashing at his legs with its powerful claws. Tucker crashed to the ground, his body convulsing in agony as blood poured from the gashes. His vision darkened at the edges, the world spinning as he struggled to breathe, his strength fading.

The creature stood over him, its gaze unwavering as it watched his life ebb away. Tucker's last, desperate attempt to crawl away was met with a swift, brutal bite, severing his leg in one savage twist. The pain was blinding, his mind barely able to comprehend the extent of his injuries as he lay helpless, his blood seeping into the earth.

With one final, ragged breath, Tucker went still, his body slumping in the grass as the life drained from him.

The creature remained for a moment, breathing heavily, its body tense as it surveyed the bloody remains of the two humans who had caused his sister's death. For a brief moment, its gaze softened as it turned back toward the lifeless form of its sibling, lying still and broken on the forest floor.

As the creature drew near, it moved with a haunting grace, dropping to all fours and lowering its massive head to nuzzle her gently, emitting a soft, mournful whine. It lingered beside her, its fury momentarily softened by a sorrow that settled deep within its chest.

Then, with one last, lingering look at the clearing, it turned and melted back into the woods, disappearing into the dense underbrush. The mist closed around it, swallowing its form as it silently left the clearing behind.

Twists you won't see coming. Suspense you'll never forget. Download _Savage Rogue_ for <u>FREE</u> with Kindle Unlimited!